AN OCCUPIED GRAVE

A BROCK & POOLE MYSTERY

A.G. BARNETT

ODDMOOR PRESS

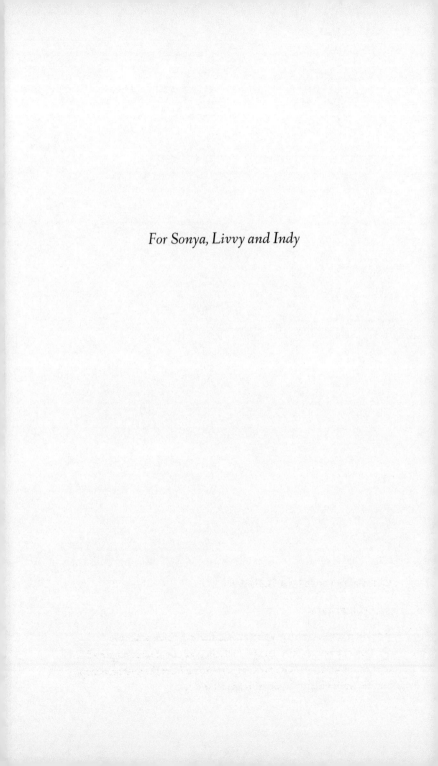

For Sonya, Livvy and Indy

A.G. BARNETT'S NEWSLETTER

For news on upcoming books visit agbarnett.com and join A.G.Barnett's newsletter to get new release alerts.

CHAPTER 1

The small group of mourners filed out of the arched doorway from the church and along the path behind the vicar. It was a grey, damp day that seemed to have covered the world in a veil for the occasion.

A crow circled above the group, fighting against the light rain. It released a low, sorrowful call as it swooped to the safety of the trees at the back of the graveyard.

The mood had shifted amongst the small congregation. They had gone from the sense of duty of paying their respects, to wanting to get the whole thing over and done with.

The drizzle from above seemed to fill the air. It attacked the group at a right angle, sneaking under the assorted black umbrellas as they shuffled along the path to the graveside. There were not enough of them to circle the grave completely, so they bunched together on one side. Opposite, the simple coffin was laid on the wet grass, ready to be lowered into the large hole which had been dug in the sodden earth.

Kate Haversham watched the vicar wipe his glasses for the third time since leaving the safety of the church. She let her eye drift across the pathetic congregation. Was this all a life amounted to? Five or six people who didn't really know you gathered in the rain and hoping for a lump of cheese on a cocktail stick afterward?

Well, there wasn't going to be any of that. There would be no wake for Edie Gaven. Not that it would have been worth it anyway with the terrible turnout. She turned her head, looking around the sloped graveyard. There were still no signs of the one person who should have been here and wasn't. She sighed and looked down into the gaping hole of the grave.

Poor Edie. The village she had lived in all her life had abandoned her. So, apparently, had her grandson.

Something caught her eye in the black gloom. A small piece of soil had shifted in the downpour, revealing the pale white skin of an elbow. Something gave way in her chest. She tried to scream but nothing came out. She turned to her husband Paul and grasped his arm.

"It's OK, love," he said, squeezing her arm in sympathy.

"No, you bloody idiot!" Kate screamed, her husband's incompetence being the only thing that guaranteed to snap her out of her horror. "There's a bloody body in there!"

"No, dear," Paul said, smiling sweetly and patting the back of her hand. "They haven't put her in yet."

"That's what I'm saying, you bloody cretin! There's a body already in there!"

The mourners leaned in as one toward the hole. A man on her right shouted and pointed toward the arm. They all saw it now. Frozen in terror, they all turned to the vicar, waiting for him to lead them in a response to this horrific news.

They watched him bend to his knees, his hands grasping the edge of the hole as he peered down into the gloom.

"I think," he said, leaning farther in, "that someone should call the police."

The earth gave way under his hands and he slipped forward, tumbling into the darkness toward the pale arm.

Detective Sergeant Guy Poole stared at the building in front of him. It wasn't much to look at. The side of the building was cold, grey concrete. The lack of effort to beautify the building was telling. This was a functional place, built for a purpose. The mirrored windows added to this feel, hiding the interior of the building from the outside world.

The sign above the entrance which Poole guessed had meant to read 'Bexford Police Station' had had the 'P' and 'O' removed. He stared at it, wondering whether this was just a happy coincidence or if the youth of Bexford had a sense of humour.

A small reception area was visible through the plate glass automatic doors; a desk at the back wall and a few plastic seats on the right. More functionality over design. The station at Oxford hadn't been much to write home about either, but it had at least been grander and more impressive than this.

He took a deep breath and tried to shake off the nerves he was feeling. He had nothing to feel nervous about, he knew that. Yes, this was a new station in a new town in a new county, but this was still police work. This was what he had trained for, this was what he wanted. Bexford, Addervale would be no different to Oxford, Oxfordshire, other than the fact that his past wouldn't be quite so present here.

This was his chance for a real fresh start and he had worked hard for it, forgoing the usual activities of people in their early twenties in order to study, to learn, to push himself. It had worked, and now here he was: a newly qualified detective sergeant, at the age of just 25.

Although it felt like he had been waiting all his life for this moment, in reality, it had been just ten years, from the moment his life had been changed forever— from one of innocence of the world around him to one of hard reality.

This wasn't the time to relive old wounds, but it was becoming hard when in a few days there was a chance it would begin to catch up with him again.

Would all of that follow him here?

He shook his head to clear the thoughts from his mind, turned back out toward the carpark and looked at his watch again. Nine fifty. He felt uncomfortable about starting late, but that's what his instructions had been. Inspector Brock, his new superior, had wanted him to pick up the car he had been assigned first.

For someone who had walked from his new rented flat to the station for the last two mornings just to look at the place, the wait was frustrating.

This morning he had picked up the car (a blue Ford Mondeo that seemed to enjoy leaping between gears without warning) at nine as he had been instructed. He had then driven straight to the station and spent the last half an hour milling around the surrounding streets, waiting for his allotted time.

He took another deep breath, turned back toward the steps and clattered into a blur in blue.

"Oh, I'm sorry!" Poole said before he had even finished staggering backward. His natural instinct to apologise was so strong that he often even found he occasionally apologised to himself under his breath.

"No problem. I was miles away," said a light voice in a thick Yorkshire accent.

Poole looked up into an angular but beautiful face of golden-coloured skin, smiling back at him with straight, white teeth. With a sudden panic, he realised that she was dressed in a police officer's uniform, her hat tucked under her arm.

"Yes, well what's your name, Constable?" he asked, trying to sound as authoritative as possible.

"Sanders, sir," she answered, standing up a little straighter and the smile fading from her lips. "Sanita Sanders."

"I don't need to know your first name, Constable, and you should consider looking where you're going in future."

"Yes, sir," she answered, her jaw tensing.

"OK, well... carry on," Poole said, putting his hands behind his back and lifting his chin slightly.

The young woman gave a curt nod and set off up the steps toward the station.

Poole exhaled and closed his eyes. His guts squirmed with guilt at his treatment of the constable, but he clenched his fists and pushed it down inside. This is how it was going to have to be. He had never had the respect of his colleagues in Oxford for reasons relating to his past. Here though, things were going to be different. Here he had a chance to make a new name for himself. Great, he thought—his new name was going to be Pompous Twit if he carried this on.

He finally climbed the steps to the station itself, pausing for a moment to check his reflection in the window to the side of the doorway. He adjusted his tie for what must have been the hundredth time that morning and stepped through the automatic doors and into a small waiting area. He walked across the cheap blue carpet and up to the front desk which sat, curved in one corner. There was no one behind it, but a door in the back wall led to an office from which voices drifted through.

He rang the small brass bell which sat on top of the counter and waited. After a few moments, a large, pasty-looking man squeezed through the doorway and came to the counter.

"What can I do for you?" the man said, leaning on the counter heavily. Poole took a small step backward in case it gave way.

"I've been transferred here from Oxford. I'm Detective Sergeant Poole."

The man's face broke into a broad grin. "Oh, nice to meet you, sir. So you'll be working with Detective Inspector Brock then, will you?"

"That's right," Poole said.

"I've got your building pass here, sir. Just hold it against the sensors by the doors." He rifled through some unseen papers behind the desk and lifted up a small grey key fob.

"Thanks," Poole said, taking it. "Where do I..."

"Through that door on the right, straight to the end of the corridor, through the door at the end and then through the next office and through the door at the back. Then all the offices have names on them, so you should find Inspector Brock's OK." His grin widened.

"Right." Poole nodded, and turned to go, but then stopped. There was something about this man's inane grin that was bothering him. "What's your name, Constable?"

"Roland Hale, sir," the man said, the smile sliding off his face.

"Is there something funny about my arrival here, Constable Hale?"

The large man swallowed, causing his chins to wobble. "Um, no, sir. Sorry, sir." He cleared his throat and busied himself with the hidden paperwork again.

Poole turned, swiped his fob and stepped through the door. He made his way along the corridor and into an office that was full of desks lined up in rows. He felt the eyes of the dozen or so constables who were dotted around follow him across the room.

The new guy.

He had been expecting this. Moving to a new place was always going to have its difficult period, and he had steeled himself for it.

He noted Constable Sanders looking at him. She caught his eye and quickly turned back to the paperwork which sat in front of her on the desk.

Poole had almost reached the door at the far end when it opened, revealing a man with a chiselled jaw, blonde hair and blue eyes. He was roughly the same six foot two that Poole reached, but the way they filled that height could not have been more different. Poole's frame was made up of long, pointy limbs which seemed to jut out of his thin body. This man, on the other hand, was muscular and toned. The tight white shirt he wore strained over his chest.

The man paused at the entrance and looked Poole up and down. "You the new chap then?" he said in a loud, sneering voice that Poole was sure was intended to carry across the whole office.

Poole held his hand out. "Detective Sergeant Poole," he said smoothly, having practised many times over the last few weeks.

The broad-shouldered man grasped his hand like a vice, his eyes narrowing under his cropped blonde hair. "Detective Sergeant Anderson," the man said, more quietly now, his fingers squeezing down on Poole's hand like a boa constrictor.

"Nice to meet you," Poole said in as level a voice as he could manage, bearing in mind the pain that was shooting through his hand.

The man snorted with laughter as a wide grin spread across his handsome face. "Hold on, you're Brock's, aren't you?"

"If you mean, am I his new sergeant? Then the answer is yes," Poole replied, pulling his hand away and trying to stand as straight as he could.

Poole prided himself on always seeing the best in people, but this Anderson was grating on him already.

"Well good luck with that." Anderson laughed. He turned to the officer that Poole had met outside who was sitting at her desk. "Sanita, grab me and Inspector Sharp a couple of coffees, will you? There's a love." He winked at her and turned back toward the door.

Poole glanced back as Sanders stood up, looking embarrassed.

"No," Poole said quietly, but loud enough so both would hear. Sanders stopped and frowned at him. Anderson paused with his hand on the door and turned back toward the room.

"What?" he said, his voice a mixture of annoyance and surprise.

"It's not a constable's job to make tea for a sergeant," Poole continued. "They might do it if they like you, but although I've only met you briefly, that scenario seems unlikely."

Blood screamed in Poole's ears. What the hell was he doing?!

"Wha..." Anderson managed, his bright blue eyes swivelling around the room which had become strangely quiet. Eventually, his expression settled on blind fury and he advanced on Poole like an angry mountain. "And who the hell are you to be telling me what I can and can't do?!" his chest puffed out so far it almost touched Poole's.

"I'm not telling you what to do, I'm telling Constable Sanders here what she doesn't have to do. It's a subtle difference, but an important one. Now, why don't you stop making a scene and go and get your own coffee?"

Anderson's breathing became heavier, faster. His eyes bulged and his face glowed crimson. His fists clenched and his mouth opened as a click from behind broke the deathly silence of the office. The door opened behind to reveal a man that at first glance appeared to be a giant. He wore trousers that finished a couple of inches from his shoes, a white shirt that had noticeable wet patches around his armpits and a tie pulled so loose it hung like a necklace.

"Everything all right out here is it, Anderson?" the

man said as he moved around, standing between the two men.

"Yes, sir," Anderson replied between gritted teeth.

"Well that's good," the man replied, his grey eyes switching between the two of them. "And you must be Poole, eh?" he said, looking him up and down.

"Yes, sir," Poole said, panic rising in his throat. This was not the first impression he wanted to give. *Please don't let this be him, please don't let this be him.*

"Well, it's good to meet you, Poole."

He held out his hand and Poole took it. It was like shaking leather baseball glove.

"I'm Inspector Brock, so I think it's me you are looking for. Shall we go and get all of us a coffee?" he said, looking at Poole and Anderson again. "Would Inspector Sharp like one too, Anderson?"

"Um." Anderson appeared to have calmed down now, and if anything looked slightly sheepish. "No need, sir. I'll get our coffee."

"Ah, splendid. Well mine's milk and two sugars. Poole?" he said, turning to him.

Anderson opened his mouth to say that that wasn't what he meant, then closed it again.

Poole smiled. "Milk, no sugar please."

Anderson's mouth squirmed before opening. "Yes, sir," he said to Brock before trudging off with a murderous look in his eye.

"Come along then, Poole. Let's show you your desk, eh?"

"Yes, sir," Poole said, trying to subdue his grin. He

turned back to see Sanders, who had returned to her seat, smiling at him. He gave her a small wave and followed the inspector through the door.

The corridor beyond was short, with three doors on either side and one at the far end. The first door they passed situated on the left had a metal plaque attached to its surface that read:

DETECTIVE INSPECTOR SHARP

They moved on to the next door, situated on the right, which read:

DETECTIVE INSPECTOR BROCK

Brock opened the door and held it for Poole, who stepped into the small space and looked around. The office was a cramped mess of paperwork and cheap furniture. A desk sat in the middle of the small room and was covered in files and sprawling sheets of paper. A filing cabinet which looked like it had taken its fair share of abuse sat in the corner, looking forlorn. A lamp stood in the opposite one. Its lampshade was torn on one side.

"This is your desk," Brock said, gesturing toward a small, cheap-looking desk that was also covered in paperwork. "You'll need to chuck that stuff on the floor."

Poole made his way to the small desk and hovered by it awkwardly.

Away from the pleasing warmth of Constable Sanders's smile, Poole was now feeling the familiar rise of nerves deep in his gut. He had been in his new job roughly ten minutes and so far had embarrassed himself in front of Constable Sanders, and then in trying to overcompensate he had made an enemy in fellow Sergeant Anderson. Now he was sat in an office that was too small for two, even more so when one of those was the size of an international rugby player.

"So, take a seat," Brock said, gesturing at the blue office chair that was positioned by his desk, its back scuffed and the arm that raised it up and down, broken off.

He sat and turned to the inspector, who had taken his place behind the mountain of paperwork on his desk.

"I tend to let it build up a bit and then have big clear-out, just dump it all in the file room for Gerald to sort out," he gestured to the piles of paper.

Poole decided not to ask who Gerald was in case it was something he should already know and he embarrassed himself even further.

There was a knock on the door.

"Come in!" Brock barked, his face clouding as though a knock on his door was a personal insult.

"Ah, Anderson, thank you," he said, brightening as the blonde sergeant entered holding two mugs of coffee.

"No problem, sir," he said, placing them both on Brock's desk.

"One of them is Poole's, I think?" the inspector said, his face a picture of innocence.

"Yes, sir," Anderson said, lifting one of the mugs and placing it in front of Poole, who was almost sure he could hear his teeth grinding. He backed out of the room, glaring at Poole.

"You've made an enemy there," Brock said once the door had closed.

"Sorry, sir," Poole said automatically.

"Sorry? Best thing you could have done. The man's an absolute arse. The fact that you've got on the wrong side of him already makes me think that you might be all right."

The inspector surveyed the gangly figure in front of him.

"You look like you're made out of golf clubs," he said, frowning.

"Um, thank you, sir," Poole said, unsure of what else to say.

"Well, if you've finished alienating your new work-force, maybe we can get to business."

Poole smiled. Despite the inspector's gruff manner, there was something likeable about him. "I'm ready, sir," he said, putting his coffee down and sitting up straight.

"I'm sure you are, but let's finish our coffee first, eh?"

"Of course, sir." Poole picked his coffee back up.

The inspector eyed him for a moment. "I looked through your file," he continued. "Very impressive." His grey eyes seemed to be boring into the back of Poole's skull, making him feel as though he was being cavity searched with his clothes on.

"Thank you, sir."

"And I see you've taken every course that's been offered to you, aced them all."

Poole sipped at his coffee, desperate for a distraction. Although this was all true, something about the way the inspector was repeating it made him feel uncomfortable.

"And how did you get on with your fellow colleagues?"

The question threw Poole for a moment. This wasn't a job interview; he was already here. With a sickening feeling, he realised his confrontation with Anderson might have raised doubts in the inspector's mind.

"I never had any issues with them, sir," he said truthfully.

"Mmm," Brock said, scratching the untidy stubble that circled his jaw. The back of Poole's neck began to prickle.

The inspector stood suddenly and grabbed a coat that hung on a hat stand in the corner of the room.

"You have a car assigned to you already, I believe?"

"Yes, sir," Poole answered, rising from his own seat. "But it's not the best, I'm afraid." What he really meant was that he had already had several murderous thoughts about the bucket of rust currently parked outside, even on just the short ride to the station this morning. The mechanic, who worked on all the local force's cars, had told him with a chuckle that he had been given the runt of the litter.

"Has it got an engine and can I fit in it?"

Poole hesitated slightly, sizing up the inspector's large frame. One, large eyebrow rose questioningly on Brock's face and Poole answered hurriedly.

"Yes, sir."

"Then I think we'll be ok."

CHAPTER 2

"A body?" Poole said slowly.

"Yes," Brock answered

"In the cemetery, sir?"

"That's what I said, Poole."

They were leaving Bexford and heading west towards the small village of Lower Gladdock.

Addervale's lush countryside streamed past their window, high hedges and rolling fields patchworking the land on all sides.

The passenger seat of the car had obstinately refused to slide back, and so Brock's knees were pitched up by his chest. Poole swore that he could feel the entire car leaning to the left from the extra weight as he guided it along the small lanes.

"I agree," the inspector continued, "a cemetery is not the most surprising place to find a body, and neither is a funeral, which is what was happening there at the time. The difference, in this case, was apparently an extra body."

"Ah, I see," Poole said. The idea of pursuing a murderer on his first day was causing a mixture of fear and excitement that was making it hard to focus on the road ahead.

"And where was it discovered?"

"In the same grave as the woman whose funeral it was, though we're not going to be able to get much of a look at it. From what I've been told by Constable Davies, there's a vicar in there at the moment. Not that he's the most reliable source of information."

Poole blinked. "The vicar's in the grave, sir?"

"Bloody hell, Poole, yes! Is there a problem with your ears or something?"

"No, sir. Sorry, sir."

Brock grunted next him and pulled a bag of boiled sweets from his coat pocket. Poole waited patiently to be offered one, but the invitation never came.

"Funny time of year, this," Brock said, staring out of the window. "Winter's over, but spring hasn't got going yet. The old life's dead and gone, but the new life hasn't come along."

Poole wasn't sure what to make of this seasonal philosophy and didn't fancy being told off again, so he kept quiet.

The sat nav attached to the window announced that they should turn right, and Poole did so.

After another quarter of a mile, a battered sign half concealed by brambles confirmed that they were now entering Lower Gladdock. After another few minutes, the lane gave way to a wider road that looped the bottom of a pretty village green.

"The church," Brock said, pointing at a small, squat tower of stone. It rose above a pretty cemetery that sloped gently down towards the green.

Two police cars and an ambulance were parked in a semi-circle around the wooden gate that led into the cemetery and two or three sorry- (and soggy-) looking people were gathered in the middle of them.

Poole pulled the car to the side of the road a few yards away along the church wall and stepped out into a deep puddle that came over the top of his black leather shoe, filling it with muddy rainwater. He leaned against the wall, pulled his shoe from his foot and began to shake it. Brock, who had reached the back of the car, looked at him and shook his head before staring up at the church.

Poole quickly rammed his shoe back on and joined him. He stood in silence for a moment, expecting instructions of some sort, but they didn't seem to be forthcoming.

"Shall we go and see what's going on, sir?" Poole said uncertainly.

Brock nodded. "That would be a good idea, yes."

Poole turned and walked towards the small crowd, trying to compose his face into one of absolute professionalism despite the fact that his right foot was squelching as he walked.

This was it. A body found in suspicious circumstances. A scene to be looked over. People to be interrogated. He could feel the adrenaline coursing through his body.

The knot of people gathered in the middle of the space were all dressed in black. *Clearly the funeral-goers,* thought Poole. No one was crying. They were talking animatedly with each other, eyes wide as they stared across the churchyard to where white-suited crime scene figures stood in the distance.

Brock and Poole ignored the questioning eyes of the few onlookers and headed through the wooden gate, Brock nodding at the constable guarding it as he opened it for them.

As they climbed the winding path through the graveyard, the scene around the grave appeared before them. A young constable was lowering a ladder down into the hole while the ambulance crew, a couple of crime scene people and a young woman watched.

They moved to the edge of the grave and peered in. It was a sorry sight: the pale flesh of an elbow jutting from the earth at one end and the small form of a very disheveled-looking vicar curled up at the other. The young constable had just reached the bottom and was attempting to get his arm around the vicar in order to lift him up.

"Oh, bloody hell," Brock muttered. "They've sent Davies down!"

Poole guessed this was a bad thing but wasn't sure why. He looked to his right and saw the young woman who was kneeling by the edge of the grave and looking in.

Her eyes were wet with tears under a mass of wild brown hair, which hung around her defined cheekbones like curtains. He noticed that her hands were gripping the edge of the grave so tightly her fingers had sunk into the soft earth.

"Excuse me, miss," Poole ventured, moving across to her. "I think you'd be better off moving back from the hole. We don't want anyone else to fall in, do we?"

Her head snapped up to his, her eyes as black and wild as her hair. She jumped to her feet before turning and running towards the church.

Poole turned back to Brock in confusion.

"My daughter," the vicar called up from over the shoulder of the young constable who was now climbing the ladder. "She's very... sensitive I'm afraid. She'll be OK once I'm out."

"OK, Vicar, don't worry," Poole answered, staring after the figure of the girl. "She's gone to the church."

"Oh good, good," the vicar said, in a voice so soft they could barely hear him over the sound of the light rain hitting the earth.

Eventually, the constable stepped out onto the grass, where he immediately slipped on the wet grass and landed on his back with the vicar on top of him.

"Bloody hell," Brock said, shaking his head.

The ambulance crew rushed to them and helped them both up.

"Well done, Davies," Brock said. "At least you didn't drop him back into the grave, eh?"

"Thank you, sir," the constable replied, picking his hat from the floor and ramming it on his head.

"Poole," Brock said, turning to him, "follow the vicar to the ambulance and have a quick word with him before they take him away, will you? Ask him when the grave was dug and who did it."

"Yes, sir," Poole said, trying to contain his excitement. He was being given the first interview of the case. A murder case. There was no other way a body accidentally ends up in a grave like this. He couldn't imagine this small village generated enough bodies for a mistake to have been made. He followed the limping vicar back down the path with a determined look on his face.

POOLE STOOD at the back of the ambulance as the crew assessed the vicar's injuries and made the necessary preparations to ready the van for leaving.

"You're taking him into hospital?" he asked as one of the crew stepped out from the doors and moved to close them.

"Just to be on the safe side," he said brusquely. "It looks like he's just twisted his ankle, but there's a fair bit of swelling, so it's best to get it checked."

"Can I talk to him first?"

"Is it important?" He shrugged.

Poole resisted the urge to explain that uncovering a dead body that shouldn't have been there was pretty important, and instead opted for what he hoped was a stern look as he stepped up through the back doors of the vehicle.

The vicar lay on a cot to the left of the vehicle. The other ambulance worker sat on a fixed bench to the right.

"Can I have a moment alone with the vicar, please?" Poole asked him.

The man grunted and squeezed past Poole and back out of the doors, leaving Poole and the slightly soiled vicar alone. He had a crop of short white hair and a top lip that struggled to cover his sizeable teeth. His frame was thin but wiry and Poole guessed that he was actually younger than he appeared at first glance.

"I just need to ask you a few questions, Vicar. It shouldn't take too long."

"No, no, quite all right," the vicar said, giving him a weak smile. "Though there is not actually much to tell, I'm afraid."

"Can I have your name please?"

"Nathaniel Hooke."

"And you were presiding over a funeral today, I understand?"

"Yes, that's right. Mrs Gaven. Not much of a turnout, I'm afraid..."

"She was from around here though?" Poole asked.

"Oh yes, she had been in the village all her life."

The vicar looked up at the roof of the ambulance

and sighed. Poole wondered if he had also hit his head as he'd fallen into the grave.

"She was an older woman, was she?"

"Oh yes," the vicar replied, "and I'm afraid she'd been ill for some time." The vicar paused and swallowed. "Multiple sclerosis," he said, softly.

Poole nodded. "And do you know how she died?"

"Pneumonia, I believe."

Poole nodded, scribbling furiously in his small black notebook.

"And the body was spotted as the congregation gathered around the graveside, is that correct?"

"Yes," the vicar said quietly, his eyes scanning the roof of the ambulance again. "The rain must have disturbed the soil and the body...um..."

"Can I ask when the grave was dug?"

"Two days ago, I think. We have a man to take care of that sort of thing. Stan Troon, his name is. He'll be able to give you a more accurate time."

"And do you have an address for Mr Troon?"

"Stan is a bit of an odd chap. Lives out in the woods in a caravan. Nice fellow though."

Poole nodded and made more notes before pausing.

The body he had seen in the grave hadn't been an old corpse exposed by the digging of the new grave. His mind flashed back to the flash of milky white skin against the dark earth. No, that body had been put there recently, almost certainly since the grave had been dug. He circled the name Stan Troon.

"I'll need your contact details as well, of course," Poole said. The vicar nodded.

"Do you inspect the grave at all before the ceremony?"

"Well, I always check everything is in order beforehand, yes, and I looked at the grave yesterday as well, but I didn't see anything out of the ordinary."

"Did you look in it?" Poole asked, watching the vicar's expression turn to one of hurt professional pride.

"I check the surrounding area is clean and presentable. I generally don't have much call to look into the graves."

Some of the colour was returning to the vicar's cheeks and he pulled himself up into a sitting position, wincing at the pain from his ankle.

"And do you know of anyone who might have gone missing from the village over the last few days?" Poole continued.

The vicar stared at him. "Not exactly missing," he said.

"And what do you mean by that?"

The vicar sighed. "I was expecting Edie's grandson to come to her funeral."

"Her grandson? And what's his name?"

"Henry Gaven."

Poole scribbled again on his notepad.

"You suspect foul play?" the vicar asked.

Poole looked up at him. "We're not suggesting anything at this stage, sir. Just looking into all possibilities. How many people would have known about the grave being dug ready for today?"

The vicar frowned. "Well, everyone in the village, I suppose. Word gets around quickly and I'm sure that everyone knew Mrs Gaven had passed away." He looked up as though he had said something inappropriate. "When am I going to be able to continue the service? The poor woman needs to be buried."

"I think it might be best if a new grave is dug; this one's going to be tied up for some time. Thank you for your time. We'll need to speak to you again at some point. I hope your ankle's OK."

"Thank you." The vicar smiled as Poole began made his way back out of the ambulance.

He paused at the doorway. "Would you like me to go and fetch your daughter? I assume she'd want to go with you?"

"Oh no, it would be too much for her, I'm afraid. I won't be long and she'll wait in the church until I'm back."

Poole frowned, said his goodbyes and stepped out onto the road.

He nodded to the ambulance crew, showing that he was finished, and made his way to the gawky police officer who had carried the vicar out of the grave.

"Constable?"

"Yes, sir!" the young man said, spinning around so fast his helmet slipped to one side. He righted it with an automatic motion that suggested it happened a lot.

"Can you begin taking statements from the congregation? Separate them off one at a time and just go over the discovery of the body and get contact details. I doubt anyone saw much, but check anyway. Then start asking them if they've noticed anything suspicious around the graveyard at all this week if they're from here. Or anything strange in the village at all." Poole paused in thought for a moment. "And ask them if anyone has gone missing recently."

"Will do, sir!" the constable said, looking excited at being given this responsibility. He scurried off to his colleague, who guarded the small wooden gate to the cemetery from the crowd and began explaining his instructions.

Poole raised his eyes towards the graves, but there was no sign of the inspector until a movement in the corner of his eye made him jerk his head to the right.

There, on the far side of the green space, was Inspector Brock. He was bending down and staring at a crumbled part of the stone wall that surrounded the graveyard.

Poole stepped through the gate and moved along the path a little as he watched the inspector make his way back.

"Everything OK, sir?" he asked as Brock joined him on the path.

"Right as rain, Poole," he said, smiling. "Let's go and have a look at the scene, shall we?"

He turned and moved up the hill rapidly with his long stride.

"What's it looking like, Sheila?" he called into the grave as they reached it.

The ladder that had been used to fetch the vicar out was still in use. Two crime scene investigators were now in the grave, gently removing soil from around the body.

"Not a lot yet, Sam. It's going to take a while to get it out. Ronald's on his way."

This last missive was in a tone that sounded a little like a warning, and the inspector seemed to take it as such.

"Thanks, Sheila. We'll catch up later. Come on, Poole," he said, turning away. Let's see what the constables have turned up and then get on our way."

They made their way down towards the group that had now diminished, leaving only one woman. The rest had begun to file into the various cars that were dotted around the green.

"And I just don't know if I can get my mum back over here again! And now you're saying you don't even know when it's going to be!"

"It's not really our job, madam," Constable Davies stammered in reply. Poole watched his Adam's apple bob up and down like a yo-yo in his throat before he turned to them with a look of relief.

"Sirs, this is Kate Haversham, the niece of Mrs Gaven, and she's a bit miffed that the funeral's been cancelled."

"Well, luckily, I doubt your auntie's that bothered, eh?" Brock said.

The woman's face flushed red and Poole sensed she was about to launch into a tirade, so he decided to dive in with a question that had just occurred to him.

"Could you tell us why people from the village haven't come to your aunt's funeral? I believe she lived here for a number of years?"

"Ha!" the woman said, her rage switching to a new target seamlessly. "This lot couldn't care less about poor old Edie!"

"Oh," Poole said. "And why is that?"

She looked at him oddly, as though she thought this was something she thought everyone knew. "Well the accident, of course." She looked at the blank faces of the three men in front of her. "Edie's grandson Henry had a few too many and killed a lad here in the village. These buggers disowned her for it! As if it was her fault! And he hasn't even got the decency to turn up today, and after she raised him as her own an' all!"

She turned and stared behind her at a car, from which a small, pale face stared out. "I need to get my mum back to our hotel. My husband's had to go back to work and I thought I'd stay a night and give mum a little holiday."

Lovely, thought Poole. A funeral is just what you want for a few days away.

"Where are you staying?" Brock asked.

"The Bell, in the village," she said, pulling herself upright and staring at him. "We can only stay one more night, mind, so that vicar better get a move on!"

"I'm sure your convenience is the first thing in his mind," Brock said before turning away towards the car.

The woman watched the retreating figure, looking slightly confused by the whole exchange, and eventually turned back to Poole.

"Well, I hope you hurry it all up!" she said before turning on her heels and heading back towards her mother.

"Looks like we've got something to get our teeth into," Brock said as Poole reached the car.

"We need to look at this accident."

CHAPTER 3

Poole tapped away at the laptop in front of him. He had removed the stacks of paper from his desk and placed them on the floor to one side and was feeling better about the office space already.

"So," he said, looking through the file, "it looks as though Henry Gaven was convicted of death by careless driving when under the influence. Had a pretty high blood alcohol reading, by the looks of it. He was coming back from a night out in Bexford and lost control of the car as he reached the village green in Lower Gladdock. Veered up onto the grass and killed a young man who was walking his dog there. Charlie Lake." Poole looked up at the inspector. His huge hands were clasped together in front of him, his elbows planted on the desk. "Sir, it says here he was released just last week."

Brock sighed. "Well, I think we can take a guess at where he is," he said quietly.

Poole realised what the inspector meant with a bolt of shock. "You mean you think he's the body, sir?"

"Remember what Mrs Gaven's niece said? That Henry Gaven hadn't even bothered to turn up to the funeral today?"

"But that doesn't mean..." Poole countered. "I mean, if the man's OK with having a skinful and then mowing someone down, he's probably not the sort to get all weepy about his gran dying, is he?"

"Not just his gran though, Poole, she 'raised him as her own', remember," he said. "And it all seems too much of a coincidence to me that he'd be released and within a week his grandmother's dead, with a strange body in the grave, and he doesn't turn up to the funeral. Now come on, let's go and get some lunch before we get stuck into the residents."

Poole stood up and followed the inspector out of the cramped office in a daze. It had been quite a morning.

His mind drifted from murder to his new flat. He pictured it now, empty apart from the boxes containing the few meagre possessions he had. This fresh start was going to take some getting used to, but there was something more pressing he hadn't yet had time for. "Erm, sir? Could I just nip to the loo?" he said as they reached the door to the main office.

Brock grunted an affirmative as they stepped into the larger office and pointed to the door on the far side of the room. "Through there, towards the canteen and it's the first door on your left. I'll wait in reception;

there's a parcel for me there I need to pick up anyway."

Poole made his way across the room, again feeling that people were watching him. This time, though, he suspected that had more to do with this morning's excitement rather than being the new guy. He opened the door and almost walked straight into Constable Sanders.

"Sorry," he said automatically, then, realising who it was, followed up with, "Erm ..."

"Thank you for this morning, sir," she said, looking around nervously. "It was very kind of you."

"Um, not at all, Constable. Just making sure everyone follows protocol, that's all," he said.

Why on earth had he said that? Making sure everyone follows protocol! He fought the urge to run and tried to think of something else to say. Why did this woman seem to turn him into an idiot?

"So, any tips for someone just starting here?"

She smiled at him. "The food's OK, but don't eat the stew. They just throw in leftovers from the week before and hope for the best."

He laughed. "Thanks. I'll remember that," he said as she moved away.

Better, he thought, and pushed open the door to the men's toilets and stepped inside.

"Ah," a voice echoed around the tiled space. "I was hoping I'd run into you."

He looked up to see Anderson stood in front of a washbasin, staring at him in the mirror.

"And why's that?" Poole asked, trying not to sound concerned.

"I thought I should make sure that you knew your place around here," he said, turning towards Poole and advancing slowly.

"And where is my place exactly?" Poole asked, though his bladder was telling him that right now, his place should be at a urinal.

Anderson leaned in until his breath was hot on Poole's face. "It's wherever I say it is," he snarled.

"Did you have garlic for lunch?" Poole took a step back, waving his hand in front of his nose.

Anderson growled and barged past him, slamming the door as he went.

A few minutes later and Poole found Brock studying a small wooden statue in the reception area along with the overweight officer behind the counter who he had seen this morning.

"Could be a staff?" the constable said.

"No, Roland, I think it is what it looks like." He looked up as he noticed Poole approaching. "Fertility statue from my wife," he said by way of explanation. "She's abroad at the moment." He turned the object round to reveal a small, but extremely well-endowed man.

"Very, um, nice, sir," Poole said, for want of anything better.

Brock shook his head. "Come on," he said and stepped through the automated doors and into the car park. He held the statue up as they walked. "It's funny," he said, turning the object in the dim light. "They've made the wrong bit big."

Poole stared at the object. "Isn't it a fertility statue?" he asked. "Seems like they made the right bit big to me, sir."

"Think about it, Poole," Brock said, his eyes alive with playfulness as he looked down at his new sergeant.

"I'm sorry, sir, I'm not sure what you mean?"

"Ah, well," Brock said, wrapping the object back in the brown paper it came out of. "Let's grab something to eat before we get back to the village. I know a place."

"JUST HERE ON THE LEFT," Brock said, pointing at a tiny shop front with a bright yellow awning. Poole swung the car over and parked against the curb.

"Come on," Brock said. "This is probably the most important person you'll meet in Bexford."

Poole followed him into the tiny shop. A counter ran along the back with an enormous blackboard menu on the wall behind it.

"Sam! Is this him?" a woman with dark eyes shouted as they crossed the threshold. She wore a white and yellow striped apron and was currently beaming at Poole as though he was a long-lost friend. Her hair was piled up in some complicated fashion, but there was still enough of it to fall either side of her face. It hung over her large, gold hooped earrings, which twisted as she talked.

"Poole, meet Sal Bonetti," Brock said, smiling.

"Nice to meet you." Poole extended a hand over the counter, but the woman batted it away, laughing. She moved around the side of the unit and embraced him in a tight hug.

"It's very nice to meet you, Poole! But I can't call you that—only first names for us. What's yours?"

"Um, Guy."

"Guy! A wonderful name!" She hugged him again before returning to the other side of the counter. "I've made up something special for the both of you on your first day as a new team, all ready to go! Let me fetch it."

She vanished through an arch into the recesses of the shop and Poole turned to the inspector with a questioning look on his face.

Brock shrugged. "She's friendly."

"And here we are!" Sal said, returning and handing them each a torpedo-shaped package in wax paper.

"Thanks, Sal. Put it on my tab, will you? We need to get off."

"Of course! Nice to meet you, Guy!" she shouted as they turned to leave.

"Yes, you too," Poole replied somewhat timidly before darting out onto the street.

"We'll eat in the village," Brock said as they walked to the car. "It's more picturesque."

They climbed in and Poole fired up the engine. "So who do you want to talk to first, sir?"

"This chap, Troon," Brock replied, looking through the paperwork on his lap. "Where does he live? There's no known address here."

"Stan Troon, the gravedigger? Lives in the woods just outside the village, sir, in a caravan".

"To the woods it is then," the inspector said, popping another boiled sweet into his mouth without offering one to Poole.

THEY DROVE on in silence until they reached the line of trees that ran to the left of the road that led towards the village. Poole slowed as a small lay-by appeared with a footpath leading in through the tall trunks.

"Here you go," the inspector said, handing Poole one of the wax paper packages. He unravelled it to reveal a seeded roll that was bursting with filling. He began to lift the top half to see what was inside, but the inspector stopped him with a raise of his hand and a noise like a bark.

"Never look inside, Poole. It would spoil the magic."

Poole looked at him as though he was mad, but turned back to the sandwich and bit into it.

It was incredible.

The juices of meat (pulled pork if Poole was to guess), pickles and cheeses mixed together in a glorious explosion.

"Wow," Poole said when he had cleared his mouth of the first bite.

"I know," sighed the inspector. "If only I could eat one of these every day, I'd die a happy man. Unfortunately, my wife knows how bad they are for you and has me restricted to one a week."

Brock thought about Laura now. He had no idea where she was exactly, travelling around South Africa somewhere with the museum. Normally when work took her away he found himself counting down the days until she returned. Lately, it had been different. An endless array of diets, fitness regimes, ovulation charts and a schedule of lovemaking that would have had Casanova considering abstinence had given him reason to enjoy the break. Particularly as the secret he was keeping from her had started to gnaw away at him more insistently over the last few months.

Anyway, she would be back in a few days, so he was damn well going to have a sandwich from Sal's every day. Even if it meant taking the new guy.

Brock turned and watched the young man as he devoured his sandwich. This really was all he needed. For years he'd got away without having a sergeant attached to him, but now he didn't have any choice. He took another bite and turned back out of the window. He needed to just forget about it all, treat this young sergeant as though everything was normal. Damn it, it was normal!

He finished and screwed up the wrapper, stuffed it into the recess between their two seats. Poole followed suit and they both stepped out, making their way to the narrow path that led through the trees.

POOLE WATCHED the large frame of Brock stride ahead. He was still slightly mesmerised by the man's size. It was as though someone had zoomed in on him. Each part of him proportionally to the next was perfectly normal, just ... bigger. If he hadn't joined the police force, Poole was fairly sure the inspector could have played rugby for England. Even if he knew nothing about the game, he could have just walked through the opposition.

His mind returned to the case.

"Would Henry Gaven really have come back to the village if he had so many enemies here, sir?" he asked as they walked along the narrow, dirt path.

"His gran was here, Poole. People don't make the obvious choices where family are concerned."

"Yes, sir," Poole answered, his jaw tensing as the image of his father came to mind. His mobile buzzed in his pocket. He pulled it out and saw that it was his mum. Alarmed by the coincidence of the timing, he rejected it, slipped it to silent and pushed it back into his pocket. She, of course, would have said that she had "sensed his unease about his father across the void", which was exactly the kind of nonsense he didn't have time for right now. She was always a pain, but the impending release of his dad had sent her craziness into overdrive.

When he had told her yesterday that he still hadn't unpacked at his new flat, she had launched into a speech about how he was always making the wrong choices simply by making too many choices. She had explained that what he really needed was to "surrender to the void", whatever the hell that meant. She was always telling him that he was too straight-laced, too focused on fitting in with the way he thought the world needed him to be. Poole could see some truth in this diagnosis, but now he had made it to detective sergeant, well, he had to feel slightly vindicated, didn't he?

"I read his file, sir," Poole said, hoping to impress. "It looks like his parents had him very young and couldn't deal with it, so he went to live with the mother's mum, Edie Gaven. His real mum died a few years later, of cancer. His dad seems to have vanished off the radar."

Brock smiled as he strode through the dappled light that passed through the overhead trees. "I read the file too, Poole."

"Oh, yes," Poole said, feeling foolish. "Of course."

A glint of light made him look up through the trees.

"Over there, sir."

Brock followed the line of his finger until he saw the reflection. It shone off a small window set into a grubby caravan. A few yards farther on, a path led off from the main one and headed towards the small clearing where the caravan stood.

Someone clearly lived here. The clearing had been turned into a neat garden. A large vegetable patch took up most of the space, but there was also a small patch of grass on which a fire pit stood with a grill over the top. The caravan itself was parked at one end.

It had once been white, but its time in the woods had meant that a light green film now seemed to cover it completely, as though it had been dipped into a scummy pond.

They entered the clearing and Brock gestured for Poole to knock on the narrow door of the caravan. He stepped onto the metal step beneath and rapped twice. There was no answer from inside, no movement. The only sound came from the gentle tinkling of wooden wind chimes that hung from a line outside the caravan. They looked handmade, carved from sticks of all shapes and sizes, presumably from the forest floor around the clearing.

The inspector turned around and began scanning the woods around them.

"Looks like he's out, sir," Poole said, watching him.

"Maybe," Brock said. "But a man living out here on his own probably has enough sense to know when someone's coming before they get to his front door. Shout into the woods," he said, still scanning the tree line. "Say who we are and why we're here."

Poole looked from the inspector, out into the trees, and back again.

Brock leaned against the caravan, his pack of boiled sweets out again. Poole wasn't offered one, so he cupped his hands around his mouth and turned back to the woods.

"Stan Troon?" he shouted. "We're from the police. We need to talk to you about a body that was discovered in the grave of Edie Gaven."

Poole turned to the inspector, who popped a sweet into his mouth and resolutely refused to offer one again. Poole was starting to think that this was moving beyond just being impolite and becoming a bit insulting. He wasn't particularly a fan of boiled sweets, but it was the principle of the thing.

A rustle of leaves from his left made him turn to see a lean, rangy man with white hair and a beard step out from the tree line.

"Want a cup of tea?" the man said as he approached them.

"That'd be lovely," Brock answered, grinning from ear to ear.

"Sit over there then," the man said, waving a finger towards the wooden bench that was set alongside the fire pit.

Brock made his way over and sat down, still grinning as he rolled the boiled sweet around his mouth.

Poole decided to remain standing and moved to the opposite side of the fire pit, which he could now see was the rusted metal of a car wheel turned on its side.

"I always liked camping," the inspector said, picking up a stick and poking at the blackened remains within. "Getting outside under the open sky."

"This isn't camping though, is it, sir?" Poole

answered bitterly. For some reason, this place was getting under his skin.

The great outdoors, with all its bugs, thorns and flea-ridden animals, had never had much appeal to him. He felt like he needed a shower already. "Do you think he has a permit to live here? Or is it his own land?"

"No I don't, and no it ain't," the sharp voice of Stan Troon came from Poole's right. He turned to see him approaching with three mugs of tea, which he placed on an upturned barrel at the end of the bench Brock sat on. "This land comes with Rose Cottage, where Edie Gaven lived, and that's owned by the church. The vicar gave me permission to live here."

Poole looked at the man as he sat on the bench next to Brock. Despite the white hair, the man wasn't old. Poole guessed mid-fifties, though it was hard to tell due to the leathery, tanned skin of a man who lived outdoors. He wore a silver hoop in his left ear and wooden beads hung around his neck. Poole couldn't believe he wasn't wearing a coat in the current weather, but Stan Troon appeared to have gone for many thin layers instead. His face was angular, and vaguely familiar to Poole, though he had no idea where from.

"Thanks," he said, taking one of the mugs that Stan now offered to him. He looked down at the mug in front of him and tried not to show repulsion at the scum that drifted around on its dark brown surface. It looked like it had been scooped from a puddle.

"I imagine you do all right out here in these

woods?" Brock said. "Nice little veg patch, a bit of hunting no doubt."

"I got permission," Troon said sharply.

"I'm sure you have," Brock continued. "How long have you lived out here then?"

"Four years, more or less."

Brock nodded and took a sip of his tea. "This grave you dug for Edie Gaven, anything strange about it?"

Poole saw a flash of emotion cross Stan's face but was unsure whether it was sadness, fear or pain.

"Nothing strange about it," Stan said. "I dug a hole, told the vicar. He paid me. Same as always."

"And you didn't see anyone you didn't recognise around the graveyard?" Poole asked.

Stan looked up at him with eyes that, to Poole, seemed older than the rest of him. "No one I didn't recognise, no."

Poole opened the file he was holding and took the photo of Henry Gaven from it. He glanced at Brock, who nodded at him to continue.

"Do you recognise this man?"

Again Poole saw a reaction on Stan's face, but again it vanished before he could get a read on it.

"I recognise him," Stan said, leaning forward and poking the smouldering fire in front of him. "It's Henry Gaven."

There was something in the way he spoke that made Poole wonder what he knew of the young man.

"You know that he was Edie Gaven's grandson?"

"Course I do! Look, there are plenty around here

who know more about that boy than I do. Why don't you go and ask them some questions and leave me in peace?" He stood up and moved across to his vegetable patch and turned his attention to the weeds.

Poole looked at the inspector, who was draining the last of his tea. Poole took the opportunity of pouring his into a small bush behind him.

"Tell us who these people are that we should talk to and we'll leave you alone," the inspector said. He placed his mug on the arm of the wooden bench and stood.

Stan Troon stopped digging with the small trowel he held and looked back over his shoulder.

"There are some people around here who lost everything the day that boy lost control of that car. If I was you, I'd start with them."

THEY WALKED in silence back along the forest path until they reached the car, the foliage around them somehow making the quiet deeper.

"Was it just me, sir," Poole asked once they had climbed inside, "or did he seem pretty upset when we mentioned Henry Gaven?"

"He did," Brock said. "The question is, why?"

The song *Kung Fu Fighting* blasted suddenly from the inspector's pocket making Poole jump. He rolled his eyes and tried to fish it out in the tight space. "My wife's idea of a joke. I don't know how to change the bloody thing," he explained as he put the mobile to his ear. "Hello?" There was a pause before he grunted an acknowledgement and said: "We'll get there now." Then he paused again, frowning. "Is Ron there?" He sighed. "OK, see you in a minute." He turned to Poole. "Back to the church; they've got the body out."

"Is this the Ronald Smith mentioned earlier?" Poole asked as he started up the car.

"Ronald bloody Smith," Brock said bitterly. "He's the pathologist and a total and utter..."

The end of the sentence was muttered and lost as he turned away to the window. Poole used his imagination to fill in the blanks.

They pulled up again outside the church, to find there had been a fair amount of activity. A black Mercedes had taken the place of one of the squad cars on the road, and a van marked 'Pathologist' had replaced the ambulance. Up on the sloped graveyard, a small white tent had been erected to the side of the grave where white-suited figures moved silently in the damp air. Brock and Poole climbed out of the car and headed up towards the tent. Brock nodded to the uniformed officer who stood a short distance from the entrance and marched past, stepping through the one flap.

"Ah, Sam! Glad to see you made it," a small man said with a grin running from ear to ear. He was stood on the other side of a table that contained the body from the grave, a white sheet laid over it. The man himself was completely bald, apart from small tufts of white hair that sprouted from above each of his large and protruding ears. He reminded Poole of a garden gnome.

"I was interviewing a suspect," Brock said gruffly. "What are we looking at?"

"Aren't you going to introduce me to your new protégé first, Sam?" the man said, turning the full beam of his grin towards Poole. Now that he saw him straight on, he realised that there was no warmth to it. He imagined it would be the sort of smile that you saw on a crocodile just before it ate you.

"This is Poole," Brock said, waving a hand at him while moving towards the body.

"Now, now, Sam, you know that I believe patience to be a virtue," Ron said.

Brock stopped short of the table and looked up to the heavens, muttering under his breath.

"My name is Ronald Smith," the man said, extending a latex-gloved hand towards Poole. He hesitated and looked down. Had that hand just been prodding and poking at a dead body?

"Bloody hell, Ron, he doesn't want to touch your corpse hand!" Brock said exasperatedly.

Ronald turned his head to one side and said, "Quite. How rude of me."

"It's nice to meet you, sir," Poole said, nodding instead. A wave of relief swept over him as the man turned his attention back to the body.

"Well as you know, Sam, I don't like to guess at

these things. I prefer to take a more meticulous approach back at the lab."

"Yes, yes," Brock said irritably. "Sheila's already told me you've got something, so just let me have it."

"Sheila should be more careful in her assumptions," Ronald said in a level voice. He looked down at the clipboard in his hand. "We have been rather fortunate though. It appears our young man here was already in the system and his fingerprints were quite easy to take."

"Henry Gaven," Brock said, staring at the white sheet as though he could see straight through it to the corpse beneath.

Ronald's small round head jerked up towards him, the smile gone from his lips. "It does appear that way, yes," he said, the wind clearly taken from his sails. "As I say, I will still need to do a thorough investigation."

"Yes, yes," Brock said, moving to the blanket and lifting the sheet from the head of Henry Gaven.

Poole stared down at the pale face. Henry Gaven was a year younger than Poole, and he felt the sudden immediacy of death as he looked down on him. Ten years ago it could very easily have been him laid on a table like this, his eyes closed, his mouth silent forever.

"Poole?"

He looked up and realised that Brock had been talking to him.

"Come on," the inspector continued, a quizzical look on his face. "Let's go and talk to the next of kin."

Poole nodded and turned to follow him out of the tent.

"Don't worry," Ronald's whiney voice came from behind. Poole turned to see the grin firmly back on his face. "Many people struggle when looking at a murder victim."

Poole's face flushed red and he turned and left without replying.

CHAPTER 4

The Bell was the only pub in Lower Gladdock and looked as though it had been there for hundreds of years. It was located away from the main green, down a side street that led to a small playing field that had an old and rather decrepit-looking village hall built in one corner.

Poole parked the car outside the village hall and they walked the short distance back to the uneven white walls of The Bell.

Stepping inside, Brock had to stoop to avoid the low beams crisscrossing the ceiling. Poole had to stifle a laugh as he watched him. He looked like an adult entering a Wendy house.

They spotted Kate Haversham sat at a table in one corner with her frail, birdlike mother perched opposite. She was staring at her phone and sipping a gin and tonic while her mother gazed out of the window with a mineral water in front of her.

"Have you sorted out what's going to happen to my poor aunt?" she said as soon as she saw them.

"Not yet," Brock said, standing awkwardly next to their table with his head at an angle. "Can I ask exactly how you're related to Edie Gaven?" He glanced at the older woman on his left and Poole realised he was worried about how this news might upset her.

"Edie was my dad's sister," Kate answered. "Why?"

"I'm afraid I have some bad news." He looked again at the mother.

"Oh, don't worry about mother; she's away with the fairies," Kate said flatly. She narrowed her eyes at the inspector. "What's the bad news then? I mean, she's already dead, isn't she?"

"I'm afraid it's Henry..."

Her mouth slowly formed a perfect "O". "You mean that was Henry in the grave?" she squawked, her voice breaking through the soft chatter of the few men who sat at the bar. Poole could feel their eyes on the back of his neck.

"I'm afraid so," Brock answered. "Can you think of anyone who would want to hurt Henry?"

She looked at him curiously and then leaned back in her chair, looking past him to towards the bar. "Well everyone around here hated him, I know that much." She frowned. "I called Edie though and she told me that he wouldn't be coming back once he got out of prison. She was all upset about it."

"When did she tell you this?"

"This was only a couple of weeks ago, just before

she got ill. Then she went into hospital. I visited her once and then she died." She shrugged and then looked thoughtful. "I wonder if she left Henry anything? I mean, I'd get it now, wouldn't I?"

Poole noticed Brock's jaw tense. "I wouldn't know, but it sounds like it would give you a motive for murder."

She recoiled in shock, her eyes seeming to revolve in her head. "But I ... You can't think I—?!"

"We're going to need you to stay at The Bell a little longer please, just for a day or two while we determine what happened to your cousin."

She nodded dumbly and they left her sitting with her mouth slightly open.

"What do you think, Poole?" Brock asked as they headed back to the car.

"I guess when she found out her aunt had died, she could have decided to kill her cousin in the hope that she would get everything, but it seems a bit of a stretch. We already know that Edie Gaven didn't own her own place, she rented it from the church. And if she's been ill for a while I can't see her having much to pass on."

"Me neither," the inspector said, looking pleased with Poole's answer. "We'll go and have a snoop round old Edie's house soon, but first I want to talk to the people affected by that car crash." He looked at his watch. "Tomorrow though, eh?"

"Yes, sir," Poole answered, and realised with surprise that he was disappointed his first day had come to an end.

~

Poole stepped out of the car into the cool night air. As he opened the main door of his block of flats, he pulled his phone from his pocket. A further four missed calls since the one this morning. He sighed and called his mother back.

"Hi, Mum," he said when she answered.

"Guy! Where have you been?!"

"At work, remember? New job, new place, etc?"

"Are you really telling me you haven't had five minutes to call me and tell me you're OK all day?"

"Actually, yes," Guy said as he trudged up the stairs to the second floor. "There was a murder."

The silence on the other end of the line made him instantly regret filling her in on his day.

"A murder!" she screeched dramatically down the phone. "Where are you right now? I'm going to come over and bring my apothecary kit. Have you put out the crystals I gave you for your new home?"

Poole glanced at the pile of boxes that were still shoved to one end of the open-plan space. "Not yet, Mum; I haven't had a chance."

"Well, no wonder there's been a murder!" she exclaimed.

Poole pulled a carton of chicken fried rice he had bought from the Chinese down the road the night before from the fridge. He had no idea how the six crystals his mother had given him could have prevented Henry Gaven's death, particularly the one that was supposed to sit on the toilet, but he also wasn't interested.

"Look, Mum, I'm pretty tired. First day and all that."

"Tired? Have you been drinking the energy elixir I made you?"

Poole glanced at the jar of green sludge that sat on his kitchen worktop, untouched. "Yes, Mum. It's delicious."

"You bloody liar! It's awful and you know it, but it will give you energy!"

"OK, fine, I'll drink it, Mum."

"Good."

"Now can I get some sleep? I've got a big day tomorrow."

"Yes, of course, love." There was a pause and Poole could guess what was coming. "Have you heard anything?"

He stopped, a forkful of rice halfway to his mouth. "No, Mum."

"OK. You'd tell me if you did, wouldn't you?"

"Of course I would."

"I'll be over tomorrow about lunchtime. Do you think you could come back and we could have lunch together?"

"Mum, it will be my second day and I'm on a murder enquiry. What do you think?"

"Well just because someone's been murdered, it doesn't mean you can't have a social life."

Poole wondered in what world having lunch with

your mum was considered a social life, but couldn't bring himself to argue. "Look, I can't make lunch, but we'll have dinner together, OK? I'll buy us in something nice."

"OK, love. Look after yourself. Love you."

"Love you too, Mum."

He put the phone down and sighed. He wasn't sure how he felt about his mum coming to stay. He definitely didn't want her on her own at the moment, not with his dad being released in two days. But there was something about her coming here that felt like she was dragging their past along with her. This was his fresh start, his new life. Yet the fear and guilt that had stalked him for a decade were still on his trail.

Brock flicked the light in his hallway and picked up the post. He smiled as he saw a postcard from South Africa amongst the bills and leaflets asking him to donate to charity. Laura had already messaged him to say she wouldn't be able to call tonight, but a postcard was almost as good.

On the front was a picture of two elephants with their trunks entwined under the orange writing that read "South Africa". He turned it over and read the familiar looped writing of his wife.

Sam,

Saw this card as I passed a small shop.
As they are the only elephants I've
seen since I've been here, I thought
you might as well see them too!
Can't wait to get back,
Love, Laura.

HE SMILED AGAIN, feeling a wave of longing rush through his gut, and walked through to the kitchen.

Perhaps it was because of the postcard, but the house felt suddenly empty and hollow. He knew that Laura would say that it needed the laughter of children to make it come alive. He still wasn't sure of that.

He slumped onto a stool at the breakfast bar and stared at the postcard. It had been two years now since they had started trying for a family. After six months Laura had insisted that they were both tested. "No pressure, no blame," she had said; it was, "just best to know where we stand".

He had known. They had told him that he had slow swimmers and that his chances of ever fathering a child were slim to none. He had told Laura that everything was fine and had been racked with guilt ever since.

He had to tell her. He would, as soon as she got back. He closed his eyes and pictured her disappointment, her anger, and worst of all, her sadness.

He shook off these depressing thoughts and moved across to the fridge. Inside was a selection of ready-made salads that he was supposed to have taken for lunch. In the freezer there lurked healthy meals for him to microwave. Laura had chided him that he would be incapable of sticking to the healthy diet she had had them on for months now. He closed the fridge, pulled his phone from his pocket and dialled the local curry restaurant. Laura had been right.

Once ordered, he slumped back down at the breakfast table with a large glass of merlot and stared at the wall. Now his thoughts turned to Poole. This was stupid. Why had he felt so bloody nervous all day? Why was he seeing the timing of this murder case as a bad omen? Was he really starting to believe all the rubbish they said about him? The "Cursed Detective" nonsense?

He rubbed his face with his hands and moved through to the front room where he sat down and flicked the TV on. The theme tune to *Foul Murder* blared out and he immediately changed the channel. "Bloody Ronald Smith," he said to no one.

CHAPTER 5

"So who do you want to talk to first, sir?" Poole turned the engine off and unclipped his seatbelt. They were back in the village of Lower Gladdock. Poole had parked against the small patch of grass opposite the church.

Despite the tower being a squat affair, it seemed to loom against the moody sky as though they were part of the same angry beast.

The weather had changed from a threatening cloud to a torrent of rain that bounced off the tarmac around the car so high that it looked like it was raining up as well as down.

"Run through them again," the inspector said, leaning his head back on the low headrest and staring up. In order to do this, he had had to slide farther down his seat and his knees were now in danger of hitting the roof of the car.

"The Lakes, parents of Charlie Lake, who was

killed in the accident; the Pagets, whose daughter was a friend of his; and the vicar's daughter, Sandra, who was also his friend apparently."

"Well let's follow the order you've got them in, Charlie Lake's parents first, then the Pagets, and we'll finish with the vicar's daughter."

Poole nodded. "The Lakes run the village shop along the road there a bit. Lower Gladdock Stores."

"Let's drive up, eh? I don't fancy spending more time than I have to in this bloody weather."

Poole fired the car up again, turning it around the loop that ran alongside the green and down the main street of the village. Houses lined the road, set back behind a mixture of neat driveways and gardens. The shop was only a few hundred yards farther down on the right. Poole swung the car across and parked right in front of its door. He looked through his window at the little shopfront, its lights dim behind the rain-soaked glass.

"It doesn't look like they're open, sir."

"Well, you better get out there and get knocking," Brock grumbled. "I'm guessing they live out the back, so you should be able to make them hear."

Poole stepped out of the car reluctantly. Despite the promotion, he couldn't help feeling that he was still on the bottom rung. As he stepped out, the rain hit him like a slap in the face. He dashed across to the door and knocked hard on the glass.

He pulled his collar up tight around him as he waited to shield himself from the stinging drops. He put his hands in his pockets and jigged from side to side as though he could dodge the onslaught. Just as he was about to give up and run back to the car, the light of the shop switched on. Through the streaks of water running down the doorway, he could make out a figure moving towards him.

The door opened to reveal a short man with an expressive, long face. This rubbery and changeable face was topped by what seemed to be a thousand lines across his forehead. They stretched back to his receding hairline, which was slicked back, wet. There was something about the large nose and soulful eyes that seemed to command respect. This was somewhat undone in Poole's eyes by the fact that he was wearing a beige dressing gown and bright pink fluffy slippers.

"David Lake?"

"Hello, can I help you?" he said with a cheery tone.

"My name is Detective Sergeant Poole and we'd like to ask you a few questions regarding the discovery of a body in the churchyard yesterday."

"And you thought you'd come straight to me and fit me up for it, did you?" the man said, laughing.

Poole blinked, confused by this response. "It's routine. We will need to speak to a number of people."

"Of course you will," the man said, his blue eyes glinting. "But you just thought you'd start with the usual suspects, eh?" The man's smile suggested he found all of this very amusing, but Poole had no idea why and so his face remained blank.

"Shall we just skip all this and go inside?" Brock's voice came from behind him.

Poole half turned but was nudged back as the inspector's large frame pushed past them and through the door. To Poole's surprise, the man let out a small chuckle and followed him in.

The shop was small but well stocked. A counter stood to the right of the door they had come in through, and a noticeboard filled with various local leaflets was fixed to the wall above it. As well as the walls being lined with shelves, there was a central row running down the middle of the rectangular space.

David Lake sauntered along the left-hand aisle and through a door at the back.

Brock and Poole followed him into a small sitting room where a plump, attractive woman lay on a sofa. She also sported a bathrobe.

"It's the police, Hayley."

The woman pursed her lips and nodded as she swung her legs off the sofa and sat upright. "Want a tea or anything?" she said. Her voice had the same thick London accent as her husband's.

"No thanks—we've just had one," Brock replied.

Poole cleared his throat. "Erm, actually I wouldn't mind a tea?"

"Of course, love," Hayley answered. "You look bloody soaked! Here, take your coat off and I'll hang it in the kitchen to dry."

Poole smiled appreciatively and passed her his sodden jacket.

"Might as well sit," David Lake said, gesturing to the sofa his wife had vacated. "Sorry about the dressing gown; we've just gotten out of the bath." He gave a leer at this which suggested they weren't solely getting clean. Poole felt his cheeks redden and began flicking through his notebook as a distraction.

"Did you know that Henry Gaven was released from prison just over a week ago?" Brock said.

"Yes, we did," David answered, his tone even. "And no, we weren't happy about it. Why, have you nicked him for something else?"

There was something in the way he said this that seemed almost gleeful.

"The little sod's got himself killed," the inspector replied flatly.

A smile spread slowly across David Lake's face. "Ha!" he shouted, clapping his hands together so loudly that Poole practically leapt off the sofa.

"Hayley? Sod the tea, open some bloody bubbly!"

"What you on about?" Hayley said, coming back in from the kitchen with a kettle in her hand.

"Gaven's only gone and bloody got killed, hasn't he!"

Hayley's eyes widened as her mouth broke into a perfect white smile before she exploded into a loud cackle.

"Oh, my days!" she said as her husband stood to hug her. She disappeared back into the kitchen and emerged only moments later with four glasses and a large bottle of champagne. Poole didn't know anything about the stuff, but the bottle looked expensive. He turned to the inspector, who so far had said nothing regarding the extraordinary reaction of the Lakes. His face was impassive.

"Don't mind if I do," Brock said, taking the flute that David Lake had filled in front of him. He tipped back, sending the golden liquid down his throat with an audible glugging sound. Poole left his on the table in front of him.

Brock smacked his lips. "Not a bad drop at all that."

"It's a Veuve Clicquot," David replied, beaming.

"Very nice," Brock said again, holding it up to the light before suddenly looking at David Lake with an intent stare. "Henry Gaven was murdered."

The smile froze for a moment on David's lips. Hayley hastily put her glass to her lips and drank deeply.

"Was he now?" David said. "Well, life has a funny way of making sure you get what's coming to you, don't it?"

"Sometimes," Brock answered, "but sometimes people take justice into their own hands."

The silence in the room suddenly grew heavy and Poole felt the hairs on the back of his neck rise to attention. The smile that now played on David Lake's lips felt different somehow. It was the smile of a predator. Cold, calculating and, frankly, scary.

"Well, I'm not sure how much more I can help you with, gentlemen?" David said, his voice even.

"You're probably right, for now," Brock said, rising.

"But we'll be wanting to speak to you again when the investigation is a little further along."

"I'm sure my wife and I can provide an alibi for any time you want."

"I'm sure you can too." The inspector smiled. He turned and set off down the hallway. Poole stood and began to follow when he remembered his coat.

"Erm, could I have my coat please?" he said to the couple who were now stood shoulder to shoulder in their white robes, glaring at him.

Hayley snorted and vanished through the kitchen door.

David Lake turned to him and frowned, his impressive forehead breaking into row upon row of lines.

"You should tell your boss that it's polite to call before turning up and accusing someone of murder."

Poole swallowed. There was something about his tone. Something about the way those soft eyes hard hardened to become like circles of steel in the last few minutes that was more than troubling.

"Here you go," Hayley said, appearing through the door and thrusting his coat back into his hands.

"Thank you." He turned and walked as quickly as he could back to the shop where Brock was waiting for him by the door.

"Having fun yet, Poole?" he said as he popped another boiled sweet into his mouth.

"I'm not entirely sure, sir," he answered honestly.

Brock chuckled as Poole unlocked the car. "Do you

know, I think that's pretty much how I feel all the time," Brock said.

They both dashed to the car and jumped inside quickly to escape the rain.

"So what do you think, sir?" Poole asked. What he had really wanted to say was, "What the hell was all that about?" But he thought that might not be appropriate.

"Well, I'd put good money on David Lake having a record, that's for sure," he said, leaning back in his seat and rolling the boiled sweet around his mouth.

Poole recalled Lake's tone when he had first knocked on the door and felt foolish for not realising before.

"Well, yes, sir. I mean, do you think they're good suspects?"

Brock turned to him with one raised eyebrow before shifting his gaze back to the rain-streaked windscreen.

"I think I'd like to know a little bit more about them, that's for sure. Come on then, let's go and see these Pagets."

THE PAGETS' bungalow was set back from the road with a neat, red-bricked driveway leading to it. Well-tended raised beds lined both sides of the path, and a small smart car stood outside the property that looked as though it had a weekly clean and polish. The overall feel was one of neatness and Poole approved of its simple domesticity.

He pressed the doorbell, which chimed a melodic tone that made Brock shake his head. The door was answered by a grey-haired couple wearing matching green and orange cardigans. Poole guessed the knitwear had to be homemade as it would surely be illegal to sell something that clashed that badly in an actual shop.

"Can we help you?" the man said with a pleasant smile.

"We'd like to talk to you about the body that was discovered in the church this morning," Brock said.

"Oh!" the woman said, raising her hands to her face and turning pale.

"Now, now, Marjory, be strong," the man said, pushing his pigeon chest out and putting his arm around her in a comforting manner. "I'm sorry, but I don't see why you would need to speak to us?"

"We have identified the victim as Henry Gaven," Brock continued.

There was another wail from Marjory. This time she buried her head in her husband's chest.

Poole removed his notebook and studied it, uncomfortable with the woman's reaction.

"Could we perhaps go inside?" Brock said.

"Yes, yes, of course," the man said, sounding slightly dazed. He steered his wife back into the house.

The bungalow was kitted out with beige walls, beige furniture and dim yellow lampshades that gave Poole the impression he was inside a giant sponge cake.

They were led through to the kitchen and again offered tea. Poole refused this time, but Brock requested a coffee. He perched on one of the chairs that were set around the small table and Poole sat next to him. He imagined that the inspector could only ever "perch" on furniture unless it was a king-sized bed.

Once Mrs Paget had managed to calm herself, they introduced themselves as Malcolm and Marjory. They sat across from Brock and Poole, holding each other's hands on top of the table.

Poole looked to the inspector to start questioning, but Brock smiled at him, waving a hand for him to take this one as he sipped his coffee. Poole cleared his throat unnecessarily and began, "Mr Paget, could you tell us about your daughter's relationships with Charlie Lake and Henry Gaven?"

Out the corner of his eye, Poole detected the corner of Brock's mouth rise slightly, clearly approving of this opening question.

Malcolm closed his eyes and exhaled through his nose slowly, making the nostrils on his narrow nose flare. "My daughter was friends with Henry Gaven— him and the others in their little gang."

Poole sensed something in his tone. "And you weren't happy with that?"

"No, we weren't," Malcolm said sharply. "Henry Gaven was a nasty piece of work and I didn't want him anywhere near my daughter."

Poole noted the past tense. Malcolm Paget had accepted his death very easily. The man was clearly angry; his thin, pipsqueak voice shook with emotion. Poole glanced at his wife. She trembled softly beside him, gripping his hand as though she might fall off her chair at any moment.

"And Charlie Lake? Sandra Hooke?"

Malcolm swallowed. "Charlie was a nice boy. It broke Charlotte's heart when he died. She never recovered, much like Sandra. Moved away and fell in with a bad crowd in London." He raised his chin and brought his other hand up to the table and his wife's hand. "She died two years ago from an overdose."

Marjory began sobbing heavily. Malcolm turned to her, glassy-eyed, and embraced her. The summing up of his daughter's life was short, to the point. Poole got the impression it was a rehearsed line. Maybe the only way he could get through telling it to a stranger.

"And you knew Henry Gaven had been released from prison?"

"We did," Malcolm said, his voice wavering. "Disgusting—only four years for killing a young man, causing all this wreckage." He shook his head and looked down at the table.

"And you know his body was found in the churchyard this morning?"

"Yes," he said, looking up, his eyes burning.

"Good bloody riddance!" Marjory shouted suddenly, her words spitting across the table towards them. She fell back into tears and Poole looked at Brock for guidance.

The inspector sat slowly stroking his chin, staring at

the couple opposite as though he was deciding something. He nodded, apparently to himself, and stood up. "Come along, Poole. I think we've bothered these people enough."

Poole looked between the couple and the inspector, slightly surprised, then rose himself.

They said their goodbyes and stepped outside into the early evening air. The rainstorm that had covered the village for most of the day had given way to a white sheet of cloud, giving the air a quiet, stifled feel, as though someone had covered the world in cotton wool.

"Well, Poole? Your turn," Brock asked as they stood by the car. "Thoughts?"

"I think a lot of people were hurt by the accident, like Stan Troon said, then Henry Gaven was killed within a week of being released. It can't be a coincidence."

Brock grimaced. "I don't like this, Poole. This accident has been hanging over this village for four years. It's been festering like an untreated wound, and that only ends badly. We need to find out who did this soon. If we don't, I think more people might get hurt before this is all over."

CHAPTER 6

Poole coasted around the wall of the church cemetery until they came to a large house set back to the left of the road that faced the bell tower.

Gravel crunched under the wheels of the car as Poole pulled into the driveway and passed a sign that read "The Vicarage" on faded wood.

"We might need to go easy on the vicar's daughter, sir," Poole said, remembering those frightened eyes by the graveside. "She's a bit of a troubled soul by the looks of it."

"Aren't we all, Poole?" Brock said, heaving himself out of the passenger seat.

The door of the vicarage was a deep blue and set into an open porch which was covered by two rose plants, their wiry thorns bare and foreboding in winter. The door was answered only a few moments after Poole had pressed the brass, Victorian doorbell.

"Good afternoon, officers," the vicar said, beaming at them. "How can I help you?"

"We'd like a word with your daughter," Brock said.

The smile fell from the vicar's face instantly. "Sandra? But why?"

"We heard that she was close with Henry Gaven before the accident four years ago. We thought it would be wise to speak to her," the inspector continued.

The vicar's lips turned in towards his teeth before he hobbled back into the hallway behind him. "Well, then I guess you better come in."

"How's the ankle, Vicar?" Brock asked as they followed him into the rather grand hallway.

"Oh much better, thank you; just a sprain, thank goodness. So silly of me, but I'm afraid discovering the poor soul like that gave me such a turn."

He led them into a sitting room where Poole took up position on a pale blue sofa as the vicar limped off to make them all tea. The place smelt of furniture polish and reminded Poole of afternoons at his grandparents' when they had been alive.

Brock paced about the room, sniffing a bunch of bright blue flowers in a vase on an oak sideboard. For some reason, this action surprised Poole. Brock didn't seem the flower-smelling type.

The inspector moved on, stopping at a collection of family photos arranged on the sill of the large bay window that looked out across the driveway. A woman appeared in most of them, alongside a much younger vicar and a smiling girl with a mass of brown curls.

"Your wife, Vicar?" Brock asked as the vicar returned with a tray containing a china teapot, cups and biscuits. Poole noticed the inspector's eyes following the tray across the room greedily.

"Yes," the vicar said, stopping suddenly. "That's my wife Denise. She passed away a number of years ago." His voice was hollow, sad. He took a sharp breath and turned back to the task at hand, moving across to the coffee table and placing the tray on it. He sat in an armchair and looked at them both. "I'm afraid my daughter is a very sensitive girl. She always had difficulties in that regard, but after the accident and losing two of her best friends ... Well, I'm afraid she rather separated from the world. She is happy enough, though, here and at the church—where things are familiar and I am nearby."

"And how did she feel about Henry Gaven?" Brock asked, moving across to the sofa and taking a biscuit.

"Well," the vicar said, looking affronted at the question. "I don't know, to be honest. We never spoke of him and it's been four years since he was in the village."

"Until this morning, of course," Brock said.

"Well, quite," the vicar said uncomfortably.

Poole could see that he wasn't quite over the ordeal of falling in the grave with the man.

"Can you tell me about Edie Gaven?" Brock asked.

"What would you like to know?"

"Did you ever visit her? Did your daughter?"

"Sandra?! No! Never. I, of course, went periodically. The village had ostracised her, but we are all

God's children. I performed my duties; helped her with odd bits of shopping when she wasn't feeling too well and the like."

"And you hadn't seen Henry since his release?"

"No, I'm afraid Mrs Gaven was convinced that he wouldn't come back to the village after everything that happened. That's what really sent her health downhill, of course."

"Why was she so convinced?"

"She'd received a postcard from Henry, I believe."

"A postcard?" Brock asked. "From prison?"

"I imagine someone brought it to him." The vicar shrugged.

"It seems like that accident hurt a lot of people..." Brock said. There was something about his tone that Poole found strange. He was quieter, more measured than his usual booming voice. He wondered if it was because he was in the presence of a vicar.

The vicar nodded sadly. "It tore the village apart."

"We do need to speak to your daughter, I'm afraid," Brock said.

The vicar sighed. "Please," he said, standing up, "be considerate." He left the room with a pained look on his face.

Poole looked at the inspector, wondering if he was going to share some thoughts on what they had talked about so far, but Brock was silently eating at a second biscuit and staring at the door the vicar had left by.

He returned after only a few minutes with the pale,

scared young woman Poole had seen by the graveside in tow.

"Now, Sandra, these men just want to ask you a few questions, but you can stop at any time."

She nodded and perched on the edge of the sofa like a small bird. Now that Poole could see her clearly, he saw how thin she was. Her red, long-sleeved top hung from her limbs like a sheet on a washing line. Her sunken eyes darted around the room, but never landed on either Brock or Poole's gaze.

For some reason, Poole felt that the calm atmosphere that the house had had when they'd entered now felt stilted.

"Sandra," Brock began, his voice soft and low. "Can you tell me the last time you spoke to Henry Gaven?"

Her eyes flashed up at him for a moment before returning to her hands.

"Henry went to prison," she said in a flat tone.

"Yes he did," Brock replied. "And was that the last time you saw him?"

"He killed Charlie," she said, her voice rising in volume. She looked up at the inspector, her face contorted in a mixture of confusion and rage.

"Yes," Brock answered, "but we are trying to find out who killed Henry."

She omitted a noise that could only be likened to a growl. Poole noticed that her hands were clenched at her side now.

"What happened on the night of the accident, Sandra?" Brock continued.

She began breathing hard, her chest heaving as she rocked slightly back and forth. "It was a sin," she said, her voice a hollow rasp.

"What was, Sandra? The accident?" Brock asked, his voice more urgent now.

"Yes!" she shouted back. "I ... we ... we are all God's creatures!" she cried out, her arms waving hopelessly in the air.

Her father put his arm around her, making her jump before she fell into his chest and sobbed.

"I'm sorry, Inspector, but I think that's enough for now. Come on, Sandra, I'll make you a cup of your special tea and you can relax." He stood and led his daughter from the room. Poole expected Brock to protest, but he leaned back in his seat and took another biscuit.

When the vicar returned a few moments later, he seemed paler and older than when Poole and Brock had arrived.

"I'm sorry, but she's just not ready to talk about these things."

"We'll have to talk to her again I'm afraid," Brock said. "Can you fill us in on anything else?"

The vicar stared at Brock for a moment with a hard look, as though he was going to throw the china teacup he had just picked straight at his head. Instead, he sighed and nodded as he stared at the floor, deflated.

"Sandra and Henry Gaven were friends, yes. And Charlie Lake and Charlotte Paget. The four of them grew up together, playing around the village from when they were knee-high."

"And what about the night of the crash?" Brock continued.

"I never got much out of Sandra, I'm afraid, but she came home in a terrible state that night—before the accident, I mean. I think they'd all been at The Bell in the village together earlier and there had been some sort of falling out. I rather think there was some sort of love trouble going on, I'm afraid. They were still just teenagers, after all, but I couldn't really tell you more than that."

"And the accident?"

The vicar heaved a sigh. "A terrible incident. Young Henry had gone off to Bexford after the argument apparently, become intoxicated and then driven back. He lost control and mounted up onto the green and hit poor Charlie Lake while he was walking the family dog."

The inspector looked thoughtful for a moment as he chewed on the last piece of the biscuit he had been eating. "And Henry was on his own in Bexford? Sandra and Charlotte didn't go with him?"

"No. After the argument everyone went home as far as I know, apart from Henry."

Brock nodded. "Have you seen anyone suspicious around the village recently? Anyone you didn't recognise?"

The vicar finally looked up from the floor. "Actually, there was a man I've seen a couple of times in the last week or so, a walker."

"And where was this man walking?"

"Well, I saw him on the footpath by the church, the one that comes out in the lane down to Mrs Gaven's. I thought it odd because we don't get many walkers around here, but he seemed quite serious. He had all the gear on at any rate."

"Could you describe him?" Poole asked.

"Well I think this is why I remembered him in particular: he was a very large gentleman. I'm afraid I, rather cruelly, thought that he didn't look like much of a walker. He was all wrapped up in a hat and scarf, so I couldn't tell you much more about his appearance."

Brock stood up, taking the last biscuit as he did so. "I think that will be all for now. Thank you very much, Vicar."

"Oh, oh right," the vicar said, standing up and leading them out. "I'm sorry about Sandra's reaction, but I'm afraid she is what she is these days."

"Not a problem," Brock said as they headed to the car. They climbed in as the door of the house shut.

Brock looked at his watch. "Just time for one more stop today, Poole."

POOLE PARKED the car with two wheels on the grass verge and they both entered The Bell Inn for the second time. He was slightly relieved to see no sign of

Kate Haversham and her mother, the only occupants of the pub being a few locals sat at the bar, talking in low grumbles. The inspector had ordered them two pints of real ale and they were now seated in the corner.

Poole sipped at the dark, nutty liquid in front of him rather gingerly. He had never drunk on duty before and he hadn't wanted to start now. The inspector, however, had insisted—even when Poole had pointed out that he was driving. "One won't do you any harm. It clears the cobwebs, gets you thinking properly."

Poole had resigned to choosing the weakest ale he could see from the three pumps behind the mahogany bar, and sipping at it slowly.

"So, Poole, go over what we know about this accident," Brock said before gulping a quarter of his pint in one.

"Well, Henry Gaven had been on a night out in Bexford, drank enough to be a couple of times over the limit and then hopped in his car to drive home. At the same time, Charlie Lake was out walking the family dog on the green. Gaven hit him and he died instantly."

"And the dog?"

Poole looked up from his beer, which he had been staring at while he searched his memory. "The dog?"

"You said he was walking a dog. What happened to it?"

Poole frowned. "I don't think it was mentioned anywhere in the report."

Brock shook his head. "People don't care about animals when the crap hits the fan."

Poole frowned even more deeply. Not only was he not an animal lover, but this didn't seem very relevant to the case.

"The accident is clearly key," Brock said. "There are too many coincidences for it not to be. But there are still a lot of questions. I can't help but wonder about the timing of Edie Gaven's death ..."

"You think she was murdered too! But it was pneumonia, wasn't it?"

Brock shrugged. "I want to order an autopsy before they eventually get her in the ground."

"Kate Haversham won't like that," Poole remarked.

"Relatives never do, Poole, but we have to be thorough."

There was a period of silence before the inspector spoke again.

"They waited four years. To sit on that anger for that long and still be ready to take your revenge ..." He paused and shook his head. "You've got to be bloody angry. First thing tomorrow we need to start digging into the Lakes' backgrounds."

"Yes, sir," Poole answered.

"Right," the inspector said, standing up, "let's go talk to the barman."

He made his way over to the far side of the bar, away from the three men who were lined up around the corner on the right.

"Same again?" the barman said, leaning two large

arms on the bar in front of him. He was tall and broad, with a sweep of ginger hair across his forehead and freckles across his large nose. Poole guessed him to be mid-fifties and thought he'd look more at home on a tractor than behind a bar.

"What you can tell us about Henry Gaven?"

The man nodded slowly. "Police?"

Poole pulled his warrant card out and held it in front of him. The man nodded again as the sound of barstools made Poole look across to where the three men were leaving. They called out goodbyes and vanished through the low doorway.

"What do you want to know about him?"

"Big drinker, was he?" Brock asked.

"Not really. Used to come in here on a Friday and Saturday night pretty regular."

"Were you here working at the time of the accident?"

"I was," the man said.

"And what can you remember about the night of the accident?"

"Only what anyone around here would know. He went and had a skinful in Bexford and drove home."

"And had you known him to drink and drive before?"

The man stood up and folded his arms. "Look, I only ever served the guy in here and he lived just down the road with his mum, so he always walked back. I don't know what he did any other time."

"Who were his friends? Who did he hang out with?"

He sighed and ran his hand through his hair. Poole got the impression that he was uncomfortable being asked all of this. He wondered if there was some unwritten code regarding barmen passing on information, like a priest or doctor.

"Well, Charlie Lake was his friend; that's what made the whole thing so ... Look." His eyes darted around the pub even though the place was empty apart from the three of them. He leaned forward on the bar again, this time leaning his head farther across the dark wood towards them. "There was Charlie, Henry, Sandra Hooke and Charlotte Paget. The four of them were inseparable, always knocking about together. Anyway, the night of the accident, Henry and Charlie had a big bust-up in here."

"What about?"

"No idea, but they all stormed out of here like the world had ended."

Poole's mind landed on the only surviving member of this group again: Sandra Hooke and her haunted eyes.

"And after the accident, did you see much of Charlotte and Sandra then?"

The man stood up again, looking uncomfortable. "Neither of them ever came in here again, that's for sure. Charlotte moved to London and died a couple of years ago. Drugs, apparently. She always was a bit of a wild one, was Charlotte."

Poole thought of her parents with their matching cardigans.

"And Sandra?" Brock pressed.

"She still lives with the vicar here, but she was never the same after it all. Had a mental breakdown I think, barely leaves her dad's side these days. Look, you're really better off talking to someone who knew them all better."

"And who would that be?" Brock asked.

The man shrugged. "Their parents, I guess."

Brock nodded and slapped his hand on the table. "Pay the man, Poole." He turned and headed for the door, leaving Poole fishing for his wallet.

By the time he had made it outside, the inspector was sucking on another boiled sweet and was leaning on the bonnet of the car, reading a sheet of paper.

"Left on the windscreen," he said as Poole approached, holding out the sheet of paper.

Written in an untidy hand were the words:

If you want answers, ask the Pagets who they were arguing with on Friday.

POOLE LOOKED up and down the short street that The Bell resided on, but there was no sign of anyone.

"Are we going to go back to the Pagets, sir?"

Brock rolled the sweet around his mouth for a

moment and then shook his head. "Not today. I don't like the idea of being dictated to by random notes from anonymous people. We'll get back to them right enough, but I'd rather speak to the person who left this note first and ask them why they wrote it and left it in the first place."

~

"You can write today up in the morning, you know," Brock said as they stood back in the station car park.

"I'd rather stay on top of it, sir."

"Fair enough," he said, raising his hands, palms up. "Just don't stay too late; I need you on it tomorrow. Oh, and I'll be having breakfast in the canteen if you want to join me, about eight?" The inspector leaned forward and slapped Poole on the shoulder, almost lifting him off his feet. "A good first couple of days, Poole. See you bright and early tomorrow."

Poole watched him turn and walk away towards town, feeling a warm glow from this unexpected praise. He turned and jogged up the steps to the station.

As he entered the main office, he was surprised to find it still had a number of people gathered there. A few were at their desks; some stood in pairs, talking. The atmosphere felt different though, less work-focused and buzzier. People were chatting, laughing, winding down at the end of the day.

He began to cut a path through the desks towards the office when the smell of coffee caressed his nostrils like a long-lost lover. He changed direction and headed towards the canteen. If he was going to spend the next couple of hours writing everything up, he might well need the hit. He nodded at a couple of officers who passed him in the doorway. They nodded back and began whispering to each other as soon as they had passed. He wondered how long this new guy tag would last, and moved through the door into the almost empty canteen. Almost, because the gawky young constable who Poole had spoken to that morning was at the coffee machine. He desperately mopped at the coffee that was overflowing from his cup and spreading across the surface of the table.

Poole grabbed a stack of napkins and helped him.

"Oh, thank you, sir!"

"No problem. Davies, was it?" Poole said, pleased that he had remembered the man's name.

"Yes, sir," the young man said hurriedly. He picked up his full-to-the-brim coffee and sipped at it. "Sorry about that, sir. I pressed it and nothing happened, so I pressed it again, but then I think it tried to do two cups."

His voice was whiny and nasal, his thin and awkward frame constantly moving as he grabbed the sodden napkins and threw them into the bin.

Poole placed a cup under the nozzle and pressed the button. Nothing happened, but he waited, and eventually the nozzle began to squirt the dark brown liquid into the plastic cup.

"Erm, sir?" Davies said. Poole realised he was

hovering, as though he wanted to say something to him but wasn't sure if he should.

"Everything OK, Davies?"

"Erm, yes, sir. It's just..." He looked around the canteen, his eyes lingering on the door for a moment. "Sergeant Anderson's running a book on how long you'll last under Inspector Brock," he blurted out, the words falling out of his mouth almost quicker than Poole could take them in.

Poole smiled, chuckled, and then laughed so hard that tears formed in his eyes, the stress of his first few days and the investigation pouring out of him in a moment.

"For what it's worth, sir, I think it's a load of nonsense," Davies said with a lopsided grin on his face.

"Thanks, Davies," Poole said, recovering himself and wiping his eyes. "I tell you what, why don't you put a bet on me sticking around. I'll stump up twenty quid as well, but don't tell Anderson it's my money."

Davies' grin widened even farther. "Nice one, sir! I will!"

Poole watched him bound out of the canteen with a loping gait and chuckled again to himself. This day had not been what he'd expected.

Inspector Brock was ... well, he wasn't sure what he was. He had a gruff, irritable manner but it seemed to be only a veneer. Below the surface, frequently visible, was a kind and friendly side. Then there was the general populace of the station, and the less-than-warm welcome from Anderson in particular. But if they thought that any of that was going to get him to quit then they must be out of their minds.

He was on a path, and he was going to follow it to the end.

"Erm, sir?"

The voice made him look up from the coffee he realised he had been stirring for at least two minutes. Constable Sanders was stood a little way away, her hat under her arm, her mouth curved into what looked like an apologetic smile.

"Oh, Constable Sanders, how are you?" he said, trying to come across as less frosty than he had earlier.

"Fine, sir. Um, I think you better go outside."

"Outside?" He lowered the coffee cup from his lips. "What's happened?"

"It's your car, sir." She turned and he followed her back to the office, which was suddenly largely deserted and out through reception onto the front steps of the station.

A group of people were gathered a few hundred yards away and laughter wafted across on the bitter night air. He realised with a sinking feeling that they were stood where his car was parked.

He made his way down the steps and a shout went up, sending the group scattering to other cars where they drove off hurriedly. He recognised a few of them from earlier in the office. In particular, he'd seen the large blonde head of Anderson bobbing away into the night.

His car was covered with a mass of wet toilet paper.

"I'm sorry," Sanders said next to him. "They're a bunch of idiots."

"Ah, it's OK," Poole said, smiling. "The thing was a piece of crap, so toilet roll actually makes sense."

Constable Sanders laughed next to him, a bright, musical laugh that made Poole feel slightly light-headed.

"That's a lot of toilet roll," he continued, unsure of what else to say but wanting to keep the conversation going.

"It's probably a month's supply for the whole office."

"Well, that probably depends on whether they're serving stew at the canteen or not, right?"

This time, Sanders burst into laughter with a little snort, which she instantly became embarrassed of. She held her hand to her mouth and blinked excessively.

Poole realised with a jolt of worry that he found this incredibly cute.

"Do you know where I could get a broom?" he asked, trying to deflect.

"Probably one in the cleaners' cupboard. Come on, I'll help you."

After finding the small cupboard next to the toilets, they armed themselves with brooms and buckets and headed back outside.

"Are you sure you don't just want to get off home?" he asked as they stepped back out into the cold night.

"Consider it a welcome-to-Bexford present," she said, smiling.

"Have you lived here long?"

"A couple of years," she replied. "I'm from Sheffield originally, but my family were moving the business down here so I decided to follow."

"And what's the family business?"

"We've got a restaurant, Balti Towers?"

He stopped in his tracks. "Balti Towers? I've had takeaways from there twice already!"

She laughed again, a sound that he was becoming fond of. "Well, I hope you enjoyed it?"

"It was great." He smiled. They arrived at his car and began scraping the toilet roll into buckets.

"So tell me about Inspector Brock," he asked as they set to work.

She glanced at him, giving him the impression that she was uncomfortable with the question.

"He's a lovely bloke," she answered, pulling a large lump of sodden tissue from the roof.

Poole realised nothing else was forthcoming and so decided to switch the conversation again. "So, what's Bexford like then?"

"Oh, it's all right," she said, sounding more relaxed again. "I mean, it's not quite as jumping as Sheffield, but it has its moments." She turned to him and pointed down at her bucket. "Mine's full."

They picked up their buckets and walked to the large bin at the edge of the car park, where they dumped their loads and returned to the car.

"There's a group of us from the station who get together for a drink every so often if you fancy coming?" Sanita said once they were back scraping at the car.

"Oh, thanks. That would be great," Poole answered, beaming.

"The inspector even comes sometimes," she continued.

Poole's smile froze slightly. He wasn't sure how he felt about going out drinking with his new boss. He decided to say nothing.

"I think that's probably about as good as it's going to get," he said, standing back a few moments later. "I can take it to a carwash in the morning to get rid of the bits."

They plonked their brushes into the mop buckets and surveyed their handiwork for a moment, before heading back to the station and returning the brushes and buckets to the cleaning cupboard.

"Can I give you a lift home or anything?" he said, realising he didn't want to leave her company just yet.

"No, it's fine thanks; I'm only walking round to the restaurant anyway. Mum and Dad don't seem to quite realise that I have a full-time job and still rope me in to help every so often."

"OK, well I'll see you tomorrow then," he said, smiling.

"See you tomorrow," she said in reply.

He turned away and headed back towards his car. It was only when he pulled out of the car park that he realised he was grinning from ear to ear.

CHAPTER 7

Poole woke feeling guilty. This was something that happened a lot, but this time it felt different. Generally, his thoughts revolved around his previous day's work. Had that report he'd handed in been good enough? Had he pressed that witness hard enough to ensure they had no more relevant information? Was he actually cut out for all of this or was he just wasting everyone's time on some crazy personal crusade?

Today, though, his feelings of guilt were fixed on Constable Sanita Sanders. She had helped scrape toilet roll off of his car for twenty minutes before they had both said an awkward goodbye and gone their separate ways. Yes, all they had been doing was brushing wet toilet paper off his car and shoving it into buckets, but he had enjoyed it. This was not good.

He had spent the last ten years decidedly not getting close to anyone. Yes, he had had colleagues back in Oxford. He had even thought of them as friends. They had gone out for drinks occasionally and he had been a part of it all. He had never let anyone get close to him though; he couldn't—not knowing that one day his father would be released and his life and the life of anyone who was close to him would be in danger.

Now the time he had been dreading had come. In just a few days his dad would be released, and now, of all times, he was in danger of letting someone get close to him, and bringing Sanita into the firing line.

His mobile buzzed on the kitchen counter, pulling him from his thoughts and back into reality. "Hello?" he answered sleepily.

"Guy!" his mother's voice barked down the phone. "You were supposed to call me when you got in last night!"

"Oh, sorry, Mum. I was tired."

"And are you still in bed? The early bird catches the worm, remember!"

"And if I want to eat worms for breakfast, I'll get right on that," he said, sighing. "So you're still on this waking up early thing, are you?"

"Ricardo says that our rhythms have been disrupted by modern life. He thinks we should all be getting up much earlier and then going to bed earlier."

"Right," Poole said, closing his eyes and placing his hand on his forehead. "Well he seems full of great ideas, doesn't he."

"Don't take that tone, Guy. Ricardo is a very important person in my life and you being all sarcastic is only going to throw off my peace circle."

Guy decided to avoid asking what on Earth a peace circle was and steer the conversation back to his new job. "Anyway, work is fine."

"Fine?! Is that all I get? What were the people like? Have you solved this murder yet?"

His mind instantly flashed to Sanita. There was no way he was going to tell his mum about her. "Well, there was a lot going on so I haven't really had time to properly meet everyone yet. And, no, we haven't solved the murder within twenty-four hours. They tend to be a bit trickier than that."

"Well, I told Ricardo all about it and he said he would be able to tell if someone had murdered someone because there would be a violent stain on their aura."

"Well, I'll be sure to inform the inspector that we have a stain spotter if one's required."

"There's that tone again, Guy!" she said in an admonishing tone. "Anyway, I was phoning to say that I'm going to be a little bit earlier today."

"How early?" Guy said, sitting up. He was starting to get a nasty feeling about this call.

"Well, according to the taxi driver I'll be there in about fifteen minutes. Oh, and my purse is at the bottom of my case. You couldn't be a dear and bring some money down for him, could you?"

Poole held the bridge of his nose in his free hand. "Fine. I'll see you in a minute."

He climbed out of bed and quickly brushed his teeth and threw on some clothes before jogging down the cold, echoing staircase towards the street.

His mother was already there when he got there, stepping out of a taxi wearing a long, floaty, Indian-style dress, her white-blonde hair sporting a braid on one side.

She was tanned, the local sunbeds of Oxford apparently in keeping with her otherwise all-natural existence.

"Guy!" she exclaimed, her arms stretched wide in front of her.

Poole walked straight past them and leaned in to pay the driver.

"You should have told me you were coming this early," he said, turning to her and hugging her. She smelt of incense.

"Well, that's what the phone call was for, dear," she said, shaking her head as though he was being silly. "Now come on, show me this new place of yours."

He sighed and led her up to the flat, all the way listening to her comment on how the acoustics "didn't create a harmonious atmosphere", and that the pale yellow on the walls "should have been a brighter shade to harness the life-giving nature of the sun".

As they stepped inside, Poole ignored the sigh from behind him and headed to make breakfast.

The small flat he had rented consisted of one bedroom and a lounge-diner with a small kitchen off to one side. As it stood, the place was completely bare other than his toothbrush and the three brand-new suits he had purchased for his new job. They hung on the curtain rail of his bedroom due to the lack of a wardrobe.

The rest of his things were still in boxes. In truth, he didn't have many possessions. The boxes were mostly full of things his mum had bought for his new place; cutlery, crockery and cleaning products.

For the three nights he had been here he had so far managed to avoid using any of them as he tested out the local takeaways.

His mother had also given him six crystals to promote good mental health, one of which, she had explained, was supposed to sit on the toilet. He couldn't for the life of him understand how a lump of crystal on the cistern was going to help his mental state, so they remained in one of the boxes.

"Well!" his mother said, hands on hips. "I love what you've done with the place!"

"Very funny," Poole replied, pushing the last slice of bread into the toaster and flipping the kettle on. "I've got to get going. There's toast in the toaster and the kettle's on. Make yourself at home."

He was out of the door and in his car five minutes later, weaving his way through the narrow streets of Bexford, which were largely empty at this hour. He hadn't quite got a handle on the place yet. It was technically a city but was so small that most people would have only ever referred to it as a town. Like many towns in England, its streets seem to have been laid out by a toddler with a crayon. They looped and curved in all manner of directions that made no sense to any right-thinking motorist. And although he was sure he now remembered the route to the station, he still had to rely on his sat nav to be certain.

When he arrived at the station car park, he made a point of parking in the exact spot he had parked in yesterday. It was left empty, despite being fairly close to the building, presumably because the remains of the toilet tissue still littered the ground there. Poole, though, wanted to make a point.

"Morning," he said to Roland Hale, the large man who worked the reception desk. He was staring at his phone as Poole walked in, his gaze flicking up only for a moment.

"Morning, sir," he said in a flat tone, before returning his eyes to the screen.

He found Brock in the canteen where he was sat at a small table against the far wall with Constables Davies and Sanders.

"Poole!" he bellowed as he saw him enter. "Grab yourself some breakfast."

"Morning, sir, Constables," he said, nodding at the inspector's table guests. He spun away quickly towards the counter, not because he was overly hungry, but more because he was worried he might blush at seeing Sanita. He squeezed his fist in annoyance. He had to get a grip of himself. He was a sergeant now, not some hormone-driven teenager with a school crush.

He grabbed what he thought was the safest-looking

thing at the buffet, scrambled eggs and a slice of toast, before paying a woman in a hairnet at the far end who sat behind an ancient-looking till and making his way back to the table.

"I was just telling these two that my wife's away so I'm taking full advantage of the canteen breakfasts until she's back," the inspector said, wiping up the remaining baked bean juice on his plate with a piece of bread. He leaned forward conspiratorially. "Only meal that isn't at risk of killing you in this place," he whispered. Davies and Sanders laughed as Poole forced an awkward smile.

Less than an hour ago he'd been in bed feeling guilty at having thoughts about a colleague. Now he was sat with the very object of these inappropriate thoughts as well as his boss.

"You two best get off to the Gaven place," the inspector said, looking at the two constables. "I saw Sheila heading off to her van to get sorted and I want our lot with her when she goes."

"Yes, sir," the two of them chorused. They stood and headed back towards the main office.

"Pretty, isn't she?" Brock said, leaning back in his chair.

Poole almost choked on a mouthful of eggs. "Um, sorry?"

"Sanders," Brock continued, a smile on his lips. "Nice woman, good officer."

"Oh, right. Good," Poole said, unsure of what he was supposed to say to this. He could feel a prickly heat rising up his neck and tore into his toast and eggs with a new ferocity in order to distract himself.

"They didn't make me inspector for nothing," Brock laughed. "I'm going to grab another coffee before we get to it. Want one?"

"Yes, thanks, sir."

Brock rose, chuckling to himself as Poole continued to shovel in eggs in embarrassment.

"When you've finished them, I want you to call St Luke's and ask them for a list of visitors Edie Gaven had before she died. Henry Gaven had been out for forty-eight hours before she died and I want to know if he went to see her."

Poole nodded, his mouth full of egg.

CHAPTER 8

Forty minutes after eating his breakfast at breakneck speed, Poole was on the move with Brock alongside him. They walked out of reception and headed across the station car park towards a long grey building that stood across the street.

"So, Henry Gaven didn't visit Edie?"

"No," Poole answered. "No one else from the village did either. Her only visitor was the vicar, but apparently he visits the hospital anyway as part of his duties."

"This Henry sounds like a right git," Brock said gruffly. "Not visiting the woman who raised you, even on her deathbed." He nodded at the building in front of them. "It's handy having the council offices near, but I'm bloody glad it's not in the same building. Ronald Smith is a sodding nightmare."

Poole thought back to his brief encounter with

Ronald Smith at the crime scene. "Yes, I can see that," he said slowly.

"He enjoys winding people up," Brock continued. Poole got the impression that what he really meant was that Ronald enjoyed winding the inspector up, but said nothing.

"We could do this over the phone," the inspector continued, "but he always insists on people going over to his office." He glanced at Poole. "He'll start on you soon enough. Just ignore all the nonsense and try and listen to the bits that are actually relevant to the case."

He pushed against a revolving door, just fitting into its space. Poole took the next one and stepped into a building that had the faint feel and smell of a hospital.

"Are we going to see the Pagets again today after that note on the car, sir?" Poole asked, trying to take his mind off the thought of the bodies that were probably in this place.

"All in good time. I want to follow my own line of enquiries first, then we'll start listening to random notes from strangers."

They followed a number of corridors that snaked around the building. Poole caught the odd glimpse of labs through open doors, all stainless steel and glass, with the smell of bleach in the air. They passed through into an area that was clearly more administrative. Suited men and women scurried past occasionally, clutching paperwork.

Eventually, they reached an office door that bore the name "Ronald Smith" with the title "Pathologist" underneath in block writing. Brock rapped on the wood with his enormous knuckles and waited. There was no sound from inside and Poole was about to ask if they should come back when he caught sight of the inspector's expression. His eyes were rolled up towards the ceiling and he seemed to be muttering something under his breath.

"Come in!" a voice shouted suddenly through the wood. Brock swung the door open with perhaps more force than was necessary and they both entered.

It was a bland, functional-looking office: white walls, small window to the right and a filing cabinet and bookshelf to the left. There was a strange, cheese-like smell in the room and Poole wondered, with a wrinkle of his nose, if it was Ronald himself. He sat behind the large desk, beaming at them with his lizard-like smile.

"Inspector!" he said in his whining voice. "And I see you've brought young Pond with you."

"It's Poole, sir."

"Is it really?" Ronald replied, as though he didn't believe him. He laughed as they sat in the two chairs in front of his desk.

"Come on, Ron, just give us the headlines so we can get out of here and get on with things."

"Always in a rush, Sam!" the man said, his perfectly round head shaking slightly above his squinting eyes. His nasal whine grated on Poole every time he opened his mouth. He got the impression that he was enjoying his moment with Brock as a captive audience.

"Now, quite an interesting one you've got here,

Sam. Buried in his grandmother's grave, I heard?" He shook his head again, his eyes closed. "The things some people are driven to."

Poole heard the inspector exhale slowly next to him. He guessed that he could well be driven to "something" by Ronald Smith.

"Well, he was killed by the blow to the back of his head, but other than that there's not much. The only thing the crime scene team picked up was contamination at the scene, which we've already eliminated. All we know is, we're looking for a long, rounded object. Probably a pipe or something. And it wasn't down in that hole with him. Other than that, the man was in decent shape, probably worked out a lot in prison. Stomach content showed noodles, probably from a packet or something. So, Pond," he said, switching his gaze from Brock, "have you by any chance seen the programme *Foul Murder*?"

The sudden change of topic took Poole by surprise. He opened his mouth, but before he could speak, the inspector jumped in.

"Oh, give it a rest will you, Ron," Brock said, standing up. "Come on, Poole, let's go."

"Oh, Sam, I'm sure Pond is a fan of the show. Millions are, you know. I'm sure Pond would be more than interested to know that I am a consultant for them on a whole range of matters." Ronald smiled like a lizard, thin-lipped and cold.

"I'm sorry, Ron," Poole said, standing up, "I've never heard of it. I'm sure it's a nice little hobby for you though." He turned and walked past the inspector, noticing the wide-eyed joy that was spreading across his face.

"I'll be in touch later for news on the victim's grandmother," Brock called as he slammed the door and followed Poole down the hall. "Perfect, Poole, just perfect," he said behind him softly. "And you even called him Ron! Just perfect."

"THERE's no record of him at all?"

"No, the only person I can find under that name died ten years ago," Poole answered. "I think it's safe to say that Stan Troon isn't who he says he is."

"And the only people we've talked to so far with a criminal record are Malcolm and Marjory Paget?" Brock said, the coffee cup halfway to his lips and a look of bewilderment on his face.

"That's right, sir. Apparently they were arrested at some protest or other back in the eighties."

"Well," Brock said, shaking his head slightly. "You never know people from just looking at them, do you? I mean, that fussy little house and matching cardigans? Turns out they were "fighting the man" in their youth."

He leaned forward, placing his elbows on the desk and looking over at Poole's screen.

"Are you sure that David Lake hasn't got a record?"

"No record I can find," Poole replied. "But I've got something on Charlotte Paget's death."

"Oh?" Brock said, one magnificent eyebrow arching.

"It's not much, but apparently she had been clean for quite a while before she relapsed and died."

"The Pagets said they thought she was doing better." The inspector nodded, scratching his stubble-covered chin.

"They did, and according to this rehab support group thing she was in, she was doing better. I spoke to a chap called Ian who was a leader of sorts in the group and he said he couldn't believe it when she overdosed."

Brock leaned back again and put his hands on the back of his head. "Makes you wonder, doesn't it?"

"Sir?"

"If she took the drugs herself." He stood up and stretched. "You see if you can find out anything about her death; I've got a quick call to make. Then I want us to get back to Lower Gladdock."

"Yes, sir," Poole answered, watching him go.

He turned back to his desk and stared at the screen without really seeing it. If she took the drugs herself? Suggesting someone might have killed her too?

He rubbed his face with both hands and got back to his task. It took a few calls, but he finally got through to the pathologist who had conducted the post-mortem on Charlotte Paget.

"Well, there was no doubt she died from an over-dose of heroin," the woman said, her voice full of sighs and boredom. She had agreed to go over the case, but only after Poole had waited for her to pull up her notes on the case, citing that she could barely remember all her cases this month, let alone from two years ago.

"And were there signs that she had been using for a while?" Poole asked.

"Well, that's just the thing. According to my paperwork, there were only two needle marks that were fresh. There was some old scarring, but only two that were recent."

Poole frowned. "Two needle marks," he said, more to himself than anything else.

"Yes, that struck me as odd too. I mean, clean for what must have been at least six months and then you fall off the wagon. Nothing strange about that, but dying on your second go? Seems odd to me."

"And you're sure that the two were recent?" Poole asked.

"According to my notes it looked like they were done in close proximity to each other both in location and time."

"Thank you, doctor," Poole said and placed the receiver down.

The door of the small office opened and Brock bustled in, making it feel at least half the size it had done before his arrival.

"I've just had a call with a friend of mine who works in London," he said, moving around behind his desk and grabbing his coat from the stand in the corner. "I bloody knew it rang a bell! As soon as I mentioned David Lake he started laughing. Knows all about him apparently. He was suspected of being the ringleader in a couple of robberies that turned violent, but they could never get anything concrete on him."

He put his coat on, a half smile playing on one side of his mouth.

"Let's get to Edie Gaven's house first, get the crime scene people in there, then we'll go and see what we can stir up."

THEY TURNED off from Lower Gladdock's village green down a small lane. It curved gently down a slope, the sound of the grass that grew in the middle of the lane scraping on the bottom of the car.

"If there's any damage," Brock said, listening to it, "it's on your head."

"Very generous of you, sir," Poole replied, smiling.

They were heading towards Edie Gaven's cottage, hoping to find signs that Henry had been there, which in turn could lead to clues regarding his death.

"Pull over here a moment," Brock said. He pointed to a small gap in the hedgerow that signalled the entrance to a footpath.

Poole pulled the car in as close as he could and the inspector stepped out. Poole followed suit and watched him make his way over to the opening in the hedge. Brock climbed on top of a large rock that protruded from the ground like an egg, and stared back in the direction of the village. He raised his hand and shielded his eyes from the first glints of sunlight that were peeking over the trees in the distance.

"What is it, sir?" Poole asked, coming up alongside him and standing on tiptoes in order to try and replicate the view.

"Crime scene team found some fibres that they've matched to Henry Gaven's clothing on a bit of fallen-down wall at the church. According to the map, the footpath runs from here and comes out alongside that wall, not far from the broken part."

Poole sank back down on to the balls of his feet and looked down, noticing some bike tracks in the mud.

He looked up at the inspector as the image of the large man walking around the edge of the churchyard wall came back to him.

"Is that what you were looking at when we arrived at the scene yesterday? And you told crime scene to look there?"

"Yep. There's only one gate into that churchyard because the back of it is a bit of waste ground covered in thick brambles. There was no way someone was going to risk bringing a body in through the front gate."

Poole thought about this as the inspector climbed down. "You mean because it's too overlooked by houses from the village, sir?"

"That and the street lights," Brock answered. "No street lights down the side where this footpath comes out, and the wall is low enough there that it wouldn't be too difficult to get the body over. Plus, it had the convenience of being reached from the footpath that runs off this lane. I looked up a map of the village."

Brock climbed back in the car and Poole hurriedly climbed in the other side. "Why would that have been convenient, sir? Wouldn't it have been difficult getting the body down here and then dragging it all along the footpath?"

"It's convenient if the murder occurred at Edie Gaven's house. Otherwise, you'd have to load it in a car and drive it out. There's the chance that someone could have seen the vehicle and recognised it in the village. Even then you've got to dump the body somewhere. The open grave was a chance to get rid of it, and this footpath would have given the killer access and cover."

Poole thought for a minute as he started the car and carried on down the narrow lane. "I'm guessing Henry Gaven didn't have a car? I mean, his license was revoked and he'd been in prison for four years. So if he did come back to the village, how did he get here? His grandmother can't have driven, surely?"

"I've been wondering about that too. No one from the village would have gone to pick him up, that's for sure, except maybe the vicar ... but he would have said. We should chase up local taxi companies around the prison and near to the village. The real question, though, is who was that jogger that the vicar saw a couple of times using that footpath?"

An expletive flew from Poole's mouth as he made the connection.

"Exactly," Brock said, smiling.

They continued down the track for another few hundred yards before it turned right into a yard. To the left stood a small white cottage surrounded by large bushes and trees on all sides. A squad car and a crime scene van were parked in the yard.

Poole noticed Constable Davies standing outside the main doorway. As the young constable saw them, he grinned and waved, causing the inspector to chuckle to himself.

"That Davies," he said, shaking his head. "It's a wonder he manages to get his uniform on the right way round every morning."

Poole slowed the car to a stop. "Quite isolated, sir," Poole said, looking around.

"It is. All the better for someone to hide away, eh?" Brock answered.

They stepped out of the car and made their way across the yard towards the house. As they reached the small path that led to the door through two large bushes, a woman in the familiar white suit of the crime scene team stepped out into the dawn light.

"What have we got, Sheila?" Brock asked.

"Nothing much. Fingerprints all over the place, the old lady's and your victim's. Loads of others too. We're logging them all."

"No blood?" the inspector asked, looking slightly disappointed.

"Found a few specks on a chopping board in the kitchen, but it's not much. Someone probably just cut a finger making dinner. I've sent it off to the lab anyway."

Brock grunted and headed off into the house.

Poole introduced himself to the suited Sheila, who slapped him on the arm good-naturedly and said, "Welcome aboard," before heading off to her van.

"Morning, sir," Davies said, blocking Poole as he tried to follow Brock into the house. "Lovely spot, isn't it!" Davies continued as he looked around the yard, beaming.

"Morning, Davies. Yes, lovely," Poole said hurriedly as he passed through the door into the gloom of the cottage.

Inside, a couple more suited crime scene workers were dusting and poking at things but without much enthusiasm. Brock moved like a tiger, despite having to stoop through every low doorway and duck the various wooden beams that crossed the ceilings. He darted from one room to another, before eventually ascending the stairs and looking into the two bedrooms that were there.

"He was here," he said as they both reached the second of the two bedrooms.

Poole looked around. It was clear someone had been staying in the room. The bed was unmade but used. Assorted cans of cheap lager lay dotted around the surfaces and there was a pile of dirty washing heaped in the corner. They had already seen Edie Gaven's room across the hall; a sparse and neat space. This had clearly been her grandson's bedroom.

They checked the various drawers in the room and found nothing of note. After a few minutes, they headed back downstairs and began rooting around the rest of the place more thoroughly.

Something began to occur to Poole. Aids and adaptations that had been made to the house were everywhere; a stairlift, an expensive armchair in the front room that lifted its occupant out when they wanted to get up. Adaptations to the bathroom included a large shower unit you could sit in. He listed the features to the inspector.

"Do you think she got all of that provided for her?"

"I doubt it," Brock said. "Maybe she had money put away? Let's look into it." He trailed off, distracted by something he'd seen in the kitchen.

"So, looks like we've found the postcard from Henry."

Guy moved to his side and took the small piece of card he offered to him. It was a scene of Bexford's town square he'd seen a dozen times on postcards already since he had moved to the area. He turned it over to reveal a few lines written in chicken-scratch handwriting.

> *Sorry Gran but I can't face coming back*
> *to the village. I know you'll be taken*
> *care of. I need a fresh start.*
> *I'll be in touch soon.*
> *Henry*

POOLE LOOKED up at the inspector, whose eyebrows had arched into horseshoes. Poole checked the date of the post office stamp, but it was smudged.

"I don't get it," Poole said. "He sends his grandmother a postcard saying he's not coming back, and then comes back? I mean, maybe it was because he'd heard she was ill, but then he didn't go and see her in the hospital?"

Brock said nothing, but exhaled. "Come on, let's go and see if Sheila's team have turned anything else up."

They headed back out into the yard. Poole nodded to Constable Davies, who was still soaking up the rays and smiling happily. They headed across to where the white crime scene van was parked when something caught his eye on the ground: another bike track like the one he had seen at the footpath farther up the lane. He tracked it right until it turned and headed down the track and became confused with the various vehicles that had come that way since. He followed it back and left until it reached the open archway of an old stone shed. He moved towards it and peered inside. He heard the inspector call from behind.

"Poole? What is it?"

He ignored him and pulled his phone from his pocket, clicking on the torch application. He passed its beam over the assorted canisters, rakes and scrap metal that were piled inside until it fell on a wheelbarrow.

"Sheila?" he shouted over his shoulder.

"Yes?"

He heard a voice from the direction of the van call back.

"I think you need to bring a kit over here."

Sheila and the inspector arrived at the opening together. The crime scene investigator carried a small toolbox with her and placed it on the ground carefully.

"I saw these tracks—" Poole pointed at the ground "—and noticed similar ones at the entrance to the footpath. I'm wondering if this is how the killer moved the body."

Brock stared at him with the expression of someone who has just discovered that their dog can talk. "Good thinking, Poole."

"Shall I bring it out?" Poole asked Sheila, eager to prove his theory correct.

"No, leave it a minute," Sheila said, waving him to one side as she opened her box and produced a liquid spray and a small torch. She leaned in and sprayed the liquid liberally over the wheelbarrow and surrounding area. She clicked the torch on and moved it around the inside of the shed, where streaks of light blue shone from almost every surface.

"Well," Sheila said with a sigh. "I think we've found our murder site."

CHAPTER 9

They had left the crime scene team swarming over the shed, ably led by Sheila, and had headed the car back down the track. Poole was trying desperately not to feel too pleased with himself, but it was difficult. Discovering the method the killer had used to transport the body was a nice piece of work.

"That was a good catch, Poole. I can see why you came with all those glowing references."

"Thanks, sir."

There was a pause. Poole had the feeling that Brock was working up to saying something.

"Let's go and see this Stan Troon, or whatever his name is. Something else has just occurred to me about him."

Poole was sure that this wasn't what the inspector had been about to say, but decided to roll with it and ask him to expand.

"Sir?"

"Something he said has been bothering me. He told us he knew Henry Gaven."

"I think his exact words were 'of course I know him'," Poole interjected.

"Exactly, but he also told us he had moved to the area four years ago."

Poole frowned. "And Gaven would have already been either in prison or soon on his way by then? Not long for Stan to get to know him."

"Exactly," the inspector said. "So he's either lying or forgetful and getting his dates wrong. Either way, I'd like to find out."

Brock pulled his seemingly inexhaustible pack of boiled sweets from his jacket and tossed one into his mouth. He moved to put them back and then paused.

"Want one?" he said to Poole, offering him the bag.

"Oh, thank you, sir," he answered, taking one. Truth be told, he hadn't wanted one, but the inspector's previous lack of generosity had been bothering him. He wondered, hoped that this was some sort of acceptance.

He turned the car left onto the main road out of the village and towards Stan Troon's caravan.

"Why did you want to become a police officer, Poole?" Brock said, wrenching Poole from his thoughts.

Poole's mouth opened and closed again as he searched for the answer. "I think I wanted to make a difference, sir," he answered honestly.

"A difference to what exactly?"

Poole looked across at him. "To people, sir. To their lives."

He felt his face redden at how corny this sounded, but it was the truth. Another thought occurred to him that made his stomach lurch. Was this about his father? He had always known that his background would be checked, that the inspector would have known who his father was and what had happened. He had even thought about broaching it on his first day, getting it over with. Then he had been thrown straight into a murder investigation and he had forgotten all about it.

He couldn't help but feel this was Brock's way of picking at that particular wound. Was he already wondering where Poole's loyalties lay?

He pulled the car over to the entrance of the footpath into the woods that housed Stan Troon's caravan. Another car was parked in the small lay-by, and Poole recognised it from their visit to the vicarage yesterday.

"Looks like the vicar's here," he pointed out.

"Probably getting Stan to dig another grave for Edie," Brock said, climbing out of the car. They headed into the woods as they had before, the sunlight vanishing as they moved beneath the boughs.

"Why do you think he lives out here?" Poole asked as they moved along the path.

"Who knows," Brock answered. "I can see why someone might just want to get away from it all. We're going to need backgrounds on everyone affected by the accident and their families, but we should look into Stan Troon's too."

"Yes, sir."

The noise of someone approaching came from up ahead.

"Oh, hello," Nathaniel Hooke said as he rounded the corner of the path. "I thought I heard voices."

"Hello again, Vicar," Brock answered. "Come to see Stan Troon, have you?"

"Well, I was trying to find him, yes, but he doesn't seem to be about." He looked around the woods spreading out on either side of them as if to highlight the point. "Strange, as I'd arranged for him to come and do some work at the church—there's a bush that needs removing—but he didn't turn up."

"Is he usually a bit flaky with jobs?" Poole asked.

"No. Quite the contrary; he's normally very punctual."

"We'll take a look about," Brock said, heading off.

"I need to get back to Sandra, I'm afraid," the vicar said with a concerned smile. "But do tell Stan not to worry about today when you see him. I just wanted to check he was OK. It can't be very cheery living out in the woods on your own like he does."

"Why does he live out here?" Poole asked.

"Well, from what I can gather he had been one of those traveller types before he came to the village. I think it must have stuck with him. I let him stay here as he didn't seem to have anywhere else to go." He shrugged.

Poole thanked him and they turned back down the path.

The clearing where the caravan stood was bathed in sunlight. Poole moved to the bench and the fire pit they had sat at earlier and put his hand over it.

"It's cold, sir."

Brock nodded and they moved across to the caravan itself.

Poole rapped on it and called out, identifying them as the police. There was no sound from inside, no movement.

Brock tried the handle and it opened with a creak, casting a shaft of light into the black interior.

"You can't go in there, sir!" Poole said, putting his hand on Brock's shoulder and then pulling it away as though he had touched fire.

The inspector turned to him and raised one eyebrow.

"We don't have a warrant to search his property," he continued, somewhat weakly.

"I think this would come under probable cause, Poole. He could be dead in there."

Poole's eyed widened as he nodded, not wanting to speak if that was true.

Brock pushed the door open and peered inside. The pitch-black interior yielded little information, so he stepped up into the space and looked up and down.

"Well he's not in here," he said over his shoulder.

A bed was set up to the right and a seated area with a table to the left.

"It's neat," Poole said, stepping in behind the inspector.

"Just because a man lives in the woods, doesn't mean he has to live like a pig, Poole."

"No, sir," he answered, feeling embarrassed at the implication that he was a snob.

"Look at this," the inspector said, pointing to a small photograph that was stuck to the wall by the bed. Poole stepped towards it and bent down. It was a picture of Henry Gaven.

"You were right, Poole; we need to get a warrant for this place. If Troon isn't back by tomorrow, I think we should crawl over this place."

"Why do you think he has it?" Poole said, sticking the picture carefully back to the blob of adhesive that had held it to the wall.

"No idea, but I want to ask him," Brock said before stepping out into the sunlight. Poole followed and closed the caravan door behind him. They looked around at the tree line that surrounded them.

"Do you think it's worth shouting out again, sir?" Poole asked.

"No; he knows who we are now. If he is out there watching us then he doesn't want to talk, and I don't fancy our chances of just the two of us finding him."

"You think he might have done a runner?"

Brock shrugged. "Who knows? Let's go and see someone we do know where to find, eh?"

They walked back towards the car in silence, both chewing over this new development.

"You don't think they were lovers, do you, sir?" Poole said when they were in the car and heading back towards the village. "I mean, I know there's a bit of an age difference, but..."

"Did you just use the term 'lovers', Poole? Bloody hell, this isn't a Jackie Collins novel. No, I don't think they were an item. Think about the timelines. Stan Troon, or whatever he's called, only moved here four years ago."

Poole nodded, annoyed with himself for forgetting there wouldn't have been much crossover.

He slowed the car as they moved down the main street of the village until the small wooden sign hanging above the shop came into view.

"They can't do much trade here, can they?" he said as they pulled up against the curb. "I mean, the village isn't on a through road or anything, so you're relying on the locals, and it's not that big."

"Anyone would think the bank robbery business means a nice retirement, eh?" Brock answered, chuckling as he stepped out of the car.

"Back again so soon, Inspector?" David Lake said as they entered Lower Gladdock stores. David Lake stood behind the small counter of the shop, an open folder of accounts in front of him.

"Well, it's hard to keep away when we have found a body just down the road from a man with your reputation."

David Lake's face twitched slightly before sliding into a smile. "Well, my reputation with your lot was always undeserved."

"Unproven at least," Brock said.

"Have you seen many walkers around the village recently?"

Poole glanced at the inspector. He hadn't expected this question, but he could see where he was going with it. The vicar, Nathaniel Hooke, had mentioned seeing a walker on the footpath by the church, and that was the way the killer had taken Henry Gaven's body.

David's face broke into a broad smile. "I keep myself to myself these days, Inspector."

"I looked up Henry Gaven's time in prison," Brock continued, unfazed. "Seems like he was attacked a lot. Stabbed in the shower, beaten up in the yard."

"Prisons can be a rough place, or so I've heard anyway." He smiled. "I've never had the pleasure personally."

"It's strange for someone to be targeted so much like that; almost as though someone had put the word out to make it hell in there for him."

"If someone did that," Lake said, his voice flat, "then I'd shake them by the hand. He deserved worse."

There was something in his tone that sent a chill down the back of Poole's neck. In that moment, he had no doubt that David Lake would have been capable of killing Henry Gaven.

"Maybe that's what was waiting for him when he came out?" Brock said. "He wasn't killed inside; maybe that pleasure was for someone to have outside of those walls and back in the real world."

Lake said nothing but raised his chin slightly, his eyes narrowed.

Brock moved suddenly closer to the counter. "Why was your son out walking the dog at three in the morning the night he died?"

The question hit Lake like a hammer blow. He stepped backwards, suddenly looking older than his years.

"I ... I don't know," he said uncertainly, his London accent becoming thicker. "We thought he was up in bed." He swallowed and continued in a hoarse voice, "The dog always slept in his room, so it must have needed to go out."

"And where did you find the dog after the accident?"

"He was back in Charlie's room somehow. We reckon he ran back after the accident and snuck in with all the comings and goings. Police and whatnot." His voice was distant, and for a moment Poole thought he was back there on that night, reliving it.

"When he came home from The Bell on the night he died," the inspector continued, "did he tell you he'd had a bust-up with his friends?"

"No, but we heard about it after. He came home with a face like thunder, swore at his mum and sodded off upstairs. That was the last we saw of him."

He took a deep breath and leaned on the counter.

"Inspector, I'm getting the impression you think you know something about my son's death that I don't."

"Not yet, but I have a feeling I will," Brock answered somewhat cryptically. "Maybe you should think of that when you're deciding on whether you can help us with our enquiries or not."

David Lake's eyes narrowed and Poole noticed that his hands had gripped the edge of the counter, but he said nothing as the inspector turned and left with Poole in tow.

They climbed back into the car before Poole asked the obvious. "You think the walker was something to do with David Lake?"

"I'm not sure, but according to the vicar, you don't see many walkers around here and then suddenly there's one that's hanging around for days? Not only that, he's on the footpath the killer used to dispose of the body. I've got no doubt that Lake knows all sorts of people who would be willing to help with a problem like that—for a price, of course."

"That's what you were getting at when you mentioned what had happened to Gaven in prison," Poole said thoughtfully. "You think David Lake was having him beaten up in there, but he made sure that no one went too far and killed him because Lake wanted that pleasure himself."

"That's my guess," Brock said grimly. "Wait!" he said suddenly, sitting upright and causing the car to rock with his massive frame. He burst out of the car door and began running across the street after a man on the opposite side. Poole clambered out after him and caught up just as the inspector had clamped one giant hand on the man's shoulder.

"You're the one that left the note on our car the other day. Care to explain why?"

"I... um," the man stammered. He looked up and down the street, looking terrified. "Come in here." He gestured them to a small alley between two old cottages, and the three of them stepped into its shadows. "Look, I'm sorry, but this is a small village. I don't want people thinking I'm talking to the police about things that don't concern me."

"Well?" Brock asked. "What are these things that don't concern you?"

"I do odd jobs around the area, and I was working on the Pagets' last week, fixing a bit of their guttering that was dripping. I realised on Friday that I'd left my hammer around the side of their house and thought I'd nip back and get it. When I was heading into their drive there was an almighty row going on. I couldn't see who it was at first but then I heard Malcolm say, 'Henry'... well." The man shook his head. "'I couldn't believe it. It was him, Henry Gaven as I live and breathe.'"

"And did you approach them?

"Did I heck!" the man said, his face making it clear what he thought of that idea. "I decided I'd get my hammer back the next morning and got out of there."

"And did you tell anyone that you'd seen him in the village?"

The man looked slightly shifty. "I might have mentioned it at The Bell, yeah."

"What's your name?" Brock asked. Despite this lead, Poole couldn't help but think that he seemed annoyed.

"Gerald Baker."

Brock ran his right hand through his hair and looked back down the alley towards the street. "Did you go back and get the hammer?"

"Yes," Gerald answered, frowning.

"I think, Mr Baker, that you had better take us back to your place and hand over this hammer."

POOLE NOSED the car out of the lane that led to Edie Gaven's cottage and saw the inspector on the single bench that adorned the village green. He pulled the car over and Brock hopped in.

"You gave the hammer to Sheila?" he asked.

"I did. She's going to have a look at it. She said to tell you they haven't found anything that looks like the murder weapon at the cottage."

Brock nodded. He had seemed sullen since they had spoken to Gerald Baker, remaining silent as they had gone to his house, a small mid-terrace in a row of three. They had retrieved the hammer from his garden shed where he kept his tools. He had decided to stay in the village while Poole had taken the hammer to Sheila. He hadn't known why, other than he needed some time to think. Sitting in the very place that the accident had happened all those years ago seemed as good as place as any.

"I don't think Gerald Baker's got anything to do with it," he said. "He's got no motive as far as I can tell, and I can't see a hammer being the murder weapon."

"Why not, sir?" Poole asked, wondering why he'd been asked to take the thing to Sheila if they didn't think it was related to the case.

"Ronald Smith said the object was cylindrical, like a pipe. I know the end of a hammer is rounded, but I can't see it matching the wound. Also, if the Pagets found it and whacked Henry over the head with it after they'd argued, would they just clean it and put it back where they found it? I think they'd dump it somewhere where it could never be found. Come on," he said, sighing. "Let's go and see the buggers."

"Well, we know they lied to us once, sir," Poole said, pulling the car away. "Maybe they thought that by putting the hammer back where Gerald had left it, no one would think of it as the murder weapon and not check it?"

He pulled into the driveway of the Pagets' bungalow and turned the engine off.

"Maybe," Brock answered, climbing out. "But it would still mean they picked up the hammer and took it all the way to Edie's cottage before whacking him over the head with it. Anyway, let's see what they've got to say for themselves if they're in," Brock said, his voice almost a growl. He rapped on the door and glanced back at the driveway. "No car," he added by way of explanation.

Marjory Paget answered the door wearing a dark grey skirt of a thick material and a cardigan of similarly insane colours to the one they had seen her and her husband wearing previously.

"Mrs Paget, we need to talk to both you and your husband. Is he in?"

"Um, no. He's out, I'm afraid," she said nervously.

"And is he likely to be back soon?" Brock asked. His tone was lacking the soft compassion that he had shown the last time they had spoken to the couple.

"I—I'm not sure." She looked past the two men towards the road behind, as though hoping Malcolm Paget would appear at any moment.

"Could we come inside for a moment?" Brock asked.

"I guess so," she said meekly, standing aside for them to enter. Brock and Poole exchanged glances as they moved past her into the house. There was something going on here; Marjory seemed worried.

They sat at the same small kitchen table they had done previously, but this time there was no offer of drinks. She sat opposite them, turning her wedding ring round on her finger again and again.

"Mrs Paget, I'm going to ask you the same question that I asked you yesterday. Have you seen Henry Gaven since he was released from prison?"

She looked up at him, her eyes wide. "I... we..." Her voice quivered as her head sunk towards the table.

"Yes," she said sadly. "He came to our house—our house!" she shouted. "After what he did! After what happened to Charlotte!" She broke down in tears, stood up and vanished into the kitchen.

"Shall I follow her, sir?" Poole asked.

"No, she's not going anywhere. She seems more worried about whether her husband's coming home or not."

As soon as the inspector had finished talking, Marjory Paget emerged from the kitchen with a small pack of tissues in hand. "I'm sorry about that; it's just all..." She waved her hands around in the air before slumping back into her chair.

"What did Henry Gaven want? Why did he come here?" Brock pressed.

Marjory's eyes darted around the surface of the table. "Malcolm's handling it," she said quietly.

"And where is your husband?" The inspector's tone was harder now.

"I... I don't know." She choked on another sob.

"Mrs Paget, you need to start telling us what is going on right now or you'll need to come into the station for a more formal interrogation."

Her head shot up, her expression one of shock.

"But the real reason you should tell us is for your husband's safety. He could be in danger."

Her face now was full of fear. Poole was impressed with how Brock had managed to press the right buttons.

"Henry turned up here in the middle of the night on Friday."

"What time exactly?"

"Around ten thirty."

Hardly the middle of the night as far as Poole was concerned, but from his experience of the Pagets so far, he wasn't surprised it counted as a late night for them.

"Go on," Brock said.

When she continued, she spat the words out angrily. "He was drunk! Prison hadn't changed him, clearly. Coming back after what he'd done to this village, and then drinking? He was throwing it in our faces."

The inspector said nothing.

"Well," Marjory continued, realising she had been showing a considerable amount of anger. "He was ranting and raving at first, not making any sense. He said that the accident wasn't his fault and then started crying about Charlie." She raised another tissue to her nose. "As if that's going to do any good now! With Charlie and Charlotte both gone and poor Sandra as she is... He ruined all their lives." She closed her eyes and said softly, "And ours."

"Mrs Paget, where is your husband?"

Her teeth bit her top lip. "Henry was saying all sorts of things. I'm sure he was just drunk, but..."

"But what?"

"He said that Charlotte didn't..." She closed her eyes and took a deep breath, steeling herself. "He said that she didn't overdose. He said someone killed her."

She looked up at the inspector, and Poole stared into her tear-filled eyes. He could see that she wanted it to be true. She wanted to believe that her daughter had been killed rather than had simply slipped back into a drug habit they had thought she had beaten.

"Did he say who? Provide any evidence for this?"

"He said someone would know, that we had to find out for ourselves."

"And that's where your husband has gone?"

She nodded with a small jerking movement. "He went to London. I don't even know where he's gone exactly; I don't think he even knows. I've tried calling but his phone's off."

Brock sighed heavily and stood up. "We'll look into it, Mrs Paget, but the second your husband calls or arrives back home, call us immediately. If there is anything to find, we'll find it, but this isn't a job for the public."

She nodded.

"We'll let ourselves out." The inspector moved around to her side of the table and placed a hand on her shoulder for a moment before leaving.

Back outside, Brock threw another boiled sweet into his mouth before holding the bag out to Poole.

"No, thank you," Poole said as they looked up and down the Main Street of the village, the breeze cool on their faces. There was rain in the air again.

"Let's get back to the station," he said as he looked up at the grey clouds above. "These four kids; Charlie, Henry, Charlotte and Sandra. Marjory Paget is right:

their lives ruined, and the lives of those that loved them. For what? One night of recklessness? There has to be more to it than that. There has to be."

As they climbed into the car and headed back towards Bexford, Poole couldn't help wondering about the inspector's desire to see more in all of this. That four young lives could be stopped so abruptly was an awful, shocking thing to believe and he seemed determined not to. Having something darker behind the accident would at least mean that this kind of thing didn't just happen, that it was the work of some ill mind.

Poole knew better. He knew that bad things did happen. They happened all the time. He had lived through them.

Poole glanced at the inspector as he fished out another sweet and stared back out of the window. He wondered for the first time if the inspector's thoughts were being skewed by the fact he and his wife were trying for a family.

CHAPTER 10

Poole placed the phone back in its cradle and scribbled down some notes. He leaned back in his chair and rubbed the back of his neck. He had been hunched over his laptop and phone for two hours now, but it had been worth it. He grabbed his mobile from his desk and tapped out a message to the inspector. He had been told to text when he had something worth talking about before Brock had vanished on whatever errands he had.

He slipped his notebook into his jacket pocket and stood up from the small desk, stretching his stiff limbs before opening the door onto the hallway.

At the same time as he stepped out, the door on the opposite side opened and Anderson appeared with a man who Poole hadn't seen before. Anderson's lip curled into a sneer at one end of his mouth at the sight of him, but he said nothing. Instead, he turned towards the door to the main office and opened it before stopping as the man behind him spoke.

"You must be Brock's new man," he said in a voice that sounded like a military general from a *Carry On* film. He had dark grey hair and a moustache that looked like someone had stuck a square of card to his top lip.

"Detective Sergeant Poole," he replied, offering his hand. The man shook it with two firm shakes before letting go.

"Inspector Sharp. Anderson here tells me that you're responsible for my coffee taking a long time the other day?" One eyebrow rose to seemingly indicate this was a shocking occurrence. "Don't let it happen again now, eh?" he said, turning towards the door where Anderson, who had been hovering with his hand over the door handle, was now smirking.

Poole followed them into the office and then watched them leave through the far door that led into the reception.

"Everybody's favourite, those two," a voice came from beside him. He turned to see Sanita Sanders stood at the photocopier to the right of the doorway.

"Afternoon, Constable," he said rather primly. He instantly regretting the formality of the greeting and tried to rectify it. "What's Inspector Sharp like?" he asked, trying to broach a more normal tone.

"Oh, he's OK. A bit old-fashioned, but I think he means well."

"Unlike his sergeant, eh?" Poole immediately

cursed himself mentally. Yes, Anderson was clearly a bully and a thug, but he was a colleague and above her rank. Why did he feel the need to put him down to Constable Sanders? It was unprofessional.

"I'm sorry, Constable Sanders, I shouldn't have said that. Sergeant Anderson is your superior."

"I think the problem is he's a little too superior," Sanders said, smirking. Poole couldn't help but laugh. There was something about her soft Yorkshire accent that seemed to disarm him, cutting away at the self-imposed barriers he had spent so much time carefully erecting.

"Do you want to get a coffee, Constable? You can fill me in on some background here at the station?"

"Yes, sir," she said, smiling. She turned towards the canteen and Poole followed in a bit of a daze.

He had heard the words before he had realised they were coming from his mouth. Of all the things he had considered doing in his first week at the job, asking beautiful constables to have a coffee with him was not on the list.

No, he told himself. This was appropriate. This was the kind of environment that the inspector wanted. He clearly often sat for breakfast with the constables; he had done it that morning. There was no ulterior motive here, only good team building.

As they poured their coffees in turn from the machine, he felt as though the eyes of four or five people who were dotted around the canteen were fixed on them. The back of his neck prickled with heat as he imagined the rumours of the new sergeant and the pretty constable floating around the station. He looked up as they turned back towards the room and felt foolish when he saw no one was looking.

"So what do you want to know, sir?" Sanders said as they sat at a nearby table.

"How long have you worked here?"

"I came down a couple of years ago," she said. "My parents were moving their business down here, and, to be honest, I didn't fancy working in the area I grew up; I'd have been arresting too many school friends!" She smiled and Poole returned it.

"And you like it here?"

"Love it," she said, taking a sip of coffee. "Bexford might not have as much going on as Sheffield, but it's so beautiful, and of course it has Sal's..."

"Oh, don't, I've been thinking about the sandwich I had there all day!" Poole said, laughing.

"Ah, the inspector's taken you there already then? Incredible, isn't it?"

"The best," Poole said, beaming. There was a pause in conversation as they both sipped at their coffee. Poole was surprised how at ease he felt with her. Even the small voice in back of his mind reminding him that she was a junior officer and that he should just walk away had quietened down.

"I heard that you discovered the murder site?" she said, leaning forward and placing her elbows on the tabletop.

"A lucky catch; I just noticed the wheel tracks in the mud and followed them."

"Davies thinks you're some kind of super sleuth. I think Sherlock Holmes was mentioned."

Poole looked at her mischievous smile and chuckled. "All that means is Davies is easily impressed."

"Ha! You can say that again. He's like a puppy, finding everything in the world exciting." She looked down at her cup as she wrapped her hands around it. "This time though I think he might have been at least partly right."

Poole felt panic and excitement rush through his chest. What did she mean by that?

His phone buzzed in his pocket and he pulled it out to see the inspector's name flashing up on the screen. "Sir?" he said, answering.

"Time for a quick recap and then call it a day, Poole. I'm outside." The call clicked off abruptly.

"Got to go," he said, standing. "Good talking to you, Sanders."

"You too, sir," she said. They smiled at each other for a moment before he turned and headed towards the exit, feeling at least two inches taller.

POOLE STEPPED out into the car park and looked around. There was no sign of the inspector anywhere. He was about to head out towards the main road on the far side of the tarmac when the familiar booming voice came from his left.

"Over here, Poole," Brock called. He turned to see him sat on a low metal barrier that ran along the edge of the car park to the side of the station building.

He was smoking a cigarette, holding it between the thumb and forefinger of his left hand, with its glowing tip facing in towards his palm as though he was hiding it.

"You're my right-hand man here now, Poole," he said, standing up as Poole arrived and headed along the metal barrier and away from the station. "And as such I expect your first loyalty to lie with me."

"Yes, sir," Poole answered, confused about where all of this was going.

"Good. Well, the first test of your loyalty comes right now."

Poole braced himself, his mind racing. Was this some kind of initiation? Was there some kind of corruption at the station that Brock was trying to wheedle out and he needed Poole onside?

"Under no circumstances are you to tell anyone that I am smoking this cigarette, and I expect this discretion to extend to the next three or four that I am almost certainly going to smoke before the evening is over. Is that clear?"

"Yes, sir," Poole answered, feeling slightly disappointed and relieved at the same time. "Who exactly would I tell though, sir?"

"My wife, for one thing; any of the constables ... oh, I don't know; just don't tell anyone and we'll be OK."

"Yes, sir," Poole answered again. He considered the likelihood of being interrogated by Brock's wife to be fairly remote, bearing in mind he had never met her. Particularly as she was abroad at the moment. He decided to let it slide.

"I've got some info on the case, sir," he said, trying to turn the conversation to more familiar waters.

"All in good time, Poole. I've taken you to Sal's; now it's time to take you to the second best-kept secret in Bexford."

They walked on in silence. Poole was under the impression that the inspector was not in the mood for chitchat. In any case, his thoughts were easily turned to Constable Sanders.

For ten minutes they passed through narrow lanes that seemed to lean inwards, blocking what light was left in the darkening sky. Eventually, they reached a short long building with walls leaning to one side as though drunk. A faded green sign hung over the door and two large bay windows that covered the front of the building. It read "The Mop & Bucket".

They entered through the low, beamed door and Brock pointed to an archway on the left. "Go and find a table; I'll get the first lot in."

Poole did as instructed, choosing a table for two in the corner next to a stained orange table lamp that sat on one of the large windows. The place seemed to be padded everywhere. The benches, the chairs, even the walls were covered with large sheets of thick material that had been stuffed with something or other, making them bulge. It smelt of stale beer and dust, but the place seemed busy. The maze of small booths, nooks and crannies that lined the walls was mostly full, though the lighting was so dim it was hard to tell. The amount of soft material in the place gave a dampened quality to the sound of people's voices, which put Poole in mind of the awful amateur dramatics his mother would drag him to at the theatre.

"Now," said the inspector, arriving back with two pints of an amber-coloured beer that he placed on the table reverentially. "This is called Bexford Gold."

"Looks very nice, sir," Poole said, picking up the glass.

"Whoa, whoa!" Brock waved his hand at Poole "This isn't stuff you just throw down your neck like any cheap beer you might find in the supermarket. This is something to savour. Smell it."

"Um ..."

"Just smell it, Poole."

Poole took the glass and raised it to his nose. "Smells a bit ..." He sniffed again. "Nutty."

Brock broke into a slow smile. "It is! Right, come on, have a sip."

Poole raised the glass slowly. He realised the response he was expected to give and so had prepared himself to fake enjoyment, but as soon as the liquid touched his lips he realised he wouldn't have to. It was nutty, but there was much more. The flavour of caramel, chocolate and hops exploded in his mouth.

"Wow, that is good," he said, taking another sip.

"I know," Brock said. "They brew it right here on the premises. Best pint in the country, if I'm any judge. Right, what have you found out about Charlotte Paget's death?"

Poole pulled his notebook from his pocket and laid it on the scratched table.

"There's an organisation called Next Steps. Apparently, it's some kind of group therapy where people get together to talk about the issues which led to their addictions."

"And Charlotte was in this group?"

"She was, for a full year."

"A year? Doesn't sound like it's much good to me then," Brock said, taking another huge swig. Poole noticed that he was already halfway through his drink and sipped at his again quickly.

"Actually, it sounds like it was working. She had been clean for six months and had become one of the mentors there that helped newer members." He looked up to see Brock's large brow furrowed in thought.

"Interesting. So this must have been some relapse she had?"

"If she had one ... the pathologist I spoke to sent her report over. It confirms that there were no signs of recent drug use other than the one that proved fatal and one other that was recent. No needle marks other than that apart from some old scarring. Bit of a coincidence, isn't it?"

"It is, and I don't like it," the inspector answered. "Henry Gaven goes out and gets drunk, then he drives home and mows down his best friend on the village green. He goes to jail. A little while later, Charlotte Paget dies from an overdose despite being apparently recovered from her drug addiction. Then Henry gets released from prison and is murdered within a week. The only person alive from the four friends is Sandra Hooke, who seems at least a couple of sandwiches short of a picnic."

"You think she might have had something to do with this?" Poole asked.

"Either that or she's next," the inspector answered darkly. "I spoke to my contact in London. I'd asked him to put the feelers out around David Lake, see if any of his old contacts might have been called in for a bit of extra work."

"And were they?"

"Well if they were, no one's talking about it, but I did get one name. There was a guy that Lake used to work with all the time, his right-hand man. Which is odd as apparently everyone knows him as "Hands". Don't ask me why. To be honest I don't want to know. Anyway, he's apparently a big guy, which would fit the description of the walker the vicar saw. Very loyal too apparently, so it wouldn't be surprising that Lake called him up for one last job."

"Killing Henry Gaven," Poole said.

"Exactly, or at least grabbing him so that Lake could do it himself."

"By the way," Poole continued, "I tracked down a taxi firm from Bexford who'd taken him to Lower Gladdock. They dropped him on a back road. I got them to talk me through where it was on a map and it looks like it's a few fields over from where Edie's cottage is. I'm guessing he came in that way so no one from the village saw him."

"And yet just a couple of nights later and he's running around the village and getting into an argument with the Pagets," Brock said thoughtfully.

They both stared at their drinks for a moment while they thought about this, then Brock broke the silence suddenly.

"Have you wondered why you were transferred here?"

"There weren't the opportunities in Oxford that there are here. Smaller station, more responsibility for everyone. I was told it would be good for my career."

"And did you believe that?"

Poole smiled. "No. I was moved here because of my dad."

Brock smiled back at him and nodded. "Good. I was worried for a minute that you thought being placed with me was a good thing." He swirled the remaining liquid in his glass before looking up at Poole with an intense gaze. "So you've heard all about the 'cursed detective', have you?"

Poole frowned. "The cursed detective? What's that? A film or something?"

Brock smiled, but it lacked any humour.

"No, it's not a film. It's me." He stood up and waggled his glass. "Another?"

"Yes, thank you," Poole answered, feeling like something significant had just happened, but he hadn't a clue what.

A few minutes later, Brock returned with the restored pint glasses and sat back down.

"I'm the cursed detective, Poole."

"Sir?" Poole looked up at him and felt the intense gaze of the inspector's cool, grey eyes hit him like a hammer. Poole got the impression he was being weighed up, judged somehow.

"This is dangerous work. Just look at the case right now. We're trying to catch a murderer, someone willing to take another life. Do you think they'd hesitate to get rid of one of us if they had the opportunity?" He sighed and stared at the tabletop.

"Ian Carter was an inspector, I was a sergeant. We were working a case, looking at a series of armed robberies that were happening at bookmakers. Long story short, we ended up cornering one of them and he pulled a gun. Carter got hit before the cavalry showed up and didn't pull through."

"I'm sorry," Poole said quietly.

"John Reeves was my first sergeant. We were responding to a tip-off about a possible sex slave ring and he was stuck with a knife. It nicked an artery and by the time we got him into an ambulance he was gone."

Poole said nothing. There was nothing to say.

"Before you feel too sorry for me," Brock continued, "I don't blame myself. They knew the risks of the job. I'm still the cursed detective though—" a wry smile played across his lips "—and you were stuck with me because of your dad. So now we both know where we stand, I just have one question."

Poole nodded.

"Has your dad, being who he is, ever affected your ability to do your job?"

"No," Poole answered immediately. "I haven't spoken to my dad since I was fifteen."

Brock nodded slowly and drank deeply from his pint glass.

"Good. So, what do you say that you and I show all these doubters what we can do and solve this bloody murder case, eh?"

"Yes, sir," Poole said, smiling again. He was starting to like Brock. Despite his general abrasiveness, loudness and all round grumpiness, he said what he thought and there was a lot to be said for that.

He felt a small worm of guilt starting to crawl in his stomach. He hadn't told Brock that his dad was to be released in a few days.

"It was a good catch with the wheelbarrow," Brock said.

"Thanks," Poole replied, grateful for the change in subject.

"You don't get to be detective sergeant at your age without being good, I can see that. It's been a while since I've had a sergeant. I've had to make do with Sanders and that idiot Davies. So I'm officially welcoming you to the team." He lifted his glass and clinked it against Poole's.

"Thank you, sir."

"Now go and get me another drink. My wife gets home tomorrow and it'll be all ovulation charts and peeing on sticks, so I'm making hay while the sun shines."

CHAPTER 11

P oole woke to the sound of his phone alarm with his head pounding. He risked opening his eyes and immediately regretted it. He had seemingly forgotten to close his curtains last night and sunlight was streaming in like a laser. He felt as though his retina were on fire. He shielded his eyes and with great effort pulled himself up.

He really wasn't used to drinking like he had last night. He vainly tried to remember how many Bexford Golds he'd had last night and gave up at four, though he suspected there had been more.

Poole showered for a long time, standing under the hot stream and closing his eyes, hoping his headache would subside. It didn't, but by the time he'd dressed, eaten a plate of scrambled eggs and thrown a cup of coffee down his throat, he was at least feeling better. That was until he saw his mother sat in the middle of his front room, cross-legged and wearing only lycra.

"Oh bloody hell, Mum, can't you wait until I've gone out?"

"This is my daily routine, Guy. You can't expect me to change it just because it might make your straight little world wobble for a while."

"Fine," Poole answered, feeling like a stropping teenager. "I'll just start leaving earlier."

"Well you know I'm only here for a few days," she answered. "Just until ..."

"I know," Poole answered softly, a hole opening in his gut.

Though they hadn't spoken about it, they both knew why she was there. Soon his dad would be released from prison, and neither of them knew what to expect.

Would he seek them out? Or start a new life somewhere else? Maybe even abroad?

One thing was for sure, they had to face it together.

THE STATION SEEMED different when he arrived at it an hour later. For the past couple of days, it had seemed a strange and intimidating place. Now it felt a little more like he belonged.

As he walked across the car park his phone buzzed in his pocket.

"Hello?"

"Guy, I forgot to say that you simply have to try this new juice purification diet."

"Mum," Guy said wearily. "Can we do this later? I'm just getting to work."

"Well pardon me for trying to make you live a longer, healthier life! Anyway, I've only been on it for three days and I can't believe the difference in me!"

"Like what?" He sighed as he jogged up the steps to the station.

"I feel dizzy, nauseous and weak!"

"OK..." Guy said slowly, feeling he was missing something.

"Well don't you see? That's the toxins leaving the body! I'm being purified!"

Poole nodded at Roland behind the reception desk and swiped his card to enter the office.

"Mum. Put down the banana and go and buy a pain au chocolat and a large latte and stop kidding yourself. You're feeling like that because you've eaten nothing but bloody fruit!" He shook his head as he heard the huff of annoyance from the other end of the line. "Look, I'm at work now. I'll see you later, OK?"

"OK, love," she answered in a slightly defeated tone.

Poole stopped halfway through the open plan office and closed his eyes. "It's going to be OK, Mum, all right?"

"I know, love," she answered, trying to sound brighter. "See you later."

He put the phone down and decided to head straight for the canteen. It was where he had found the inspector previously, and more importantly, it was where he'd find more coffee.

The canteen was virtually empty. Two constables sat at a table towards the till and Inspector Brock sat at the same table he had the other day. He looked up, caught Poole's eye and gestured for him to come over.

"Bloody hell, Poole," he said as he approached. "You look like you could do with a full English." He gestured down in order to indicate that that was what he had just polished off.

"I think I might actually, sir," Poole replied, feeling slightly annoyed at how unaffected Brock seemed by last night's activities.

"Well go on then and you can get me another coffee while you're there."

Poole nodded and turned away. He grabbed two coffees from the machine before loading up his plate with two sausages, two rashers of bacon, a hash brown, mushrooms, beans and two fried eggs. Then, at the last minute, he added a plate of toast to his tray as well.

He paid and then made his way back to the table, where the inspector grinned when he saw the plate of food.

"Now that's a breakfast," he said, the grin fading into a look of slight sadness. "Last day of it for me, I'm afraid," he said sourly.

Poole swallowed the mouthful he had shoved in and looked up at him. "Because your wife's getting home?"

Brock nodded. "She's got me on some diet that's

supposed to increase fertility." He sighed. "As if eating tonnes of asparagus, broccoli and walnuts is going to make any difference. The only thing it's given me is wind."

Poole laughed and almost choked on the bacon he had been in the process of swallowing. For some reason, Brock's openness didn't bother him as much anymore.

His mind turned to his father again and his impending release.

THE BELL CHIMED as Poole stepped through the door to the Lower Gladdock stores. David Lake looked up from the floor where he was knelt placing tins of beans on the low shelf in front of him.

"Well, well, well, if it isn't the police back to harass me some more about the death of my son."

"Actually, Mr Lake, we're more interested in the whereabouts of your friend Hands at the moment," Brock said. He followed Poole through the door and threw a boiled sweet into his mouth.

For the first time, it struck Poole that they were possibly a replacement for cigarettes. Either that or the inspector's wife had heard they were good for fertility.

Lake stood up and sighed. "Fair enough, Inspector, you've looked into me and found out the name of someone close to me in the old days. Excellent police work." He stared at them both for a moment, as though weighing them up.

"I don't know where Hands is at the moment," he continued. "But I can find him for you. It might not do you much good though; Hands isn't a big fan of the police."

"Then maybe you can tell us what we need to know?" Brock said. "Was Hands in the village? Did you hire him to take care of Henry Gaven?"

Lake's drooping, soulful eyes grew hard again.

"I guess you might as well know, Inspector. There's nothing that can come back on me, just in case you're getting your hopes up. Yes, I hired Hands to come down here. I knew Gaven would come back. Where else was he going to go? With his gran sick and all on her own, I knew he'd turn up."

"So you hired Hands to keep an eye out for him? And then what?"

"And then come and tell me. I wanted to handle Gaven myself."

"And did you?" Brock asked, a steel edge to his voice.

"I didn't have the pleasure, no. Hands saw him, all right, coming out of old Edie's house."

"He didn't see him going in?"

"No. We think he must have come in a back way somehow, knew people would be looking out for him."

"And where did he go when he left?"

"To Malcolm and Marjory Paget's, of all places.

Had some sort of bust-up with them, according to Hands, then he went home."

"And did Hands go there? To his gran's house?"

"Nope, he came and told me."

"And what did you do then?"

Lake laughed. "I did nothing. Like a bloody fool, I thought I had time. Next morning I heard that his Gran was dead. I wasn't sure what he'd do then. I guessed there would be nothing keeping him in the village, so I went round there. There was no one about. I guessed that he'd scarpered. That's why we were happy when you brought us the good news that the sod was dead. I thought he'd gotten away with it." David Lake's eyes filled with a mixture of anger and sadness.

"And your buddy Hands will back all this up, will he?"

"He will."

Brock smiled, but there was no warmth to it. "I'm sure he will. You should know, Lake, you've moved to the top of our suspect list," Brock said, turning towards the door.

"Lucky old me." Lake grinned.

CHAPTER 12

The Pagets' melodic doorbell rang out as they stood in the driveway in silence. They had noticed the lack of a car in the driveway, just as in their last visit. When Marjory Paget opened the door, Poole could tell by the expression on her face that Malcolm had not returned.

"Oh..." she said, her hand rising to her mouth.

"Malcolm hasn't come home?" Brock asked.

"No. He called though. He said..." The words stuck in her throat.

"What did he say, Marjory?"

"He said he'd found something. He told me to make sure all the doors were locked and that he'd be home in a few hours."

"And when was this?"

She caught another sob. "Eleven last night."

"And you haven't heard from him since?"

"No," she said in a small, terrified voice.

"Oh, hello, Inspector, Sergeant." They turned to see the vicar approaching from the road.

"Morning, Vicar. Were you looking for us?"

"Actually, no." He peered round to look at Marjory Paget. "I was just wondering if everything was all right with your car, Marjory?"

"Our car? What do you mean?" she asked, her voice rising in panic.

"Well I saw it parked on the edge of the green and wondered if something had happened. Broken down or something?" he asked, looking between the three of them with the look of a man who realised he was missing something, but without knowing what.

Marjory burst past Poole and ran down the drive to the road, where she vanished to the left.

"Get after her, Poole, and don't let her touch anything!" Brock shouted, pushing his sergeant in the back as though to emphasise the point.

Poole caught up with her well before the green and they jogged along together until they reached the cool green grass and he told her to wait.

He circled the car, carefully peering into its windows and breathing a sigh of relief when nobody appeared to be present inside.

It was pulled half up onto the grass from the road. Poole realised with a pang of annoyance that they must have passed it as they had come into the village that morning, but there was nothing to mark it as anything out of the ordinary.

"Is this your car, Mrs Paget?"

"Yes," Marjory replied shakily.

"Poole?" Brock called as he and the vicar arrived at the green. Poole looked up and shook his head, knowing somehow that the inspector was thinking the same as he had been—that Malcolm Paget may be dead inside the vehicle.

"Is there anywhere in the village your husband might have gone, Mrs Paget?"

"I... no, I don't think so." She seemed to be in a daze. The vicar approached her and took her hand lightly, at which point she fell upon his shoulder and exploded into sobs. Brock and Poole convened at the rear end of the car, putting a discreet distance between them.

"Looks like he was in a rush," Poole said, pointing to where tyre impressions weaved up onto the grass a few feet before turning back to the road again.

"I don't like the coincidence of it," Brock answered.

"Sir?" Poole looked up at him.

"Another car, on the green."

Poole realised what he meant. Four years ago a car mounting the green had been the cause of so much anguish in this little village and had possibly resulted in the more recent death of Henry Gaven.

"Get the crime scene guys on this, and get a uniform out here to take a formal statement from Mrs Paget. And tell them to hurry up as we need to go."

"Go where, sir?" Poole said, pulling his phone from his pocket.

"Well, Malcolm Paget isn't the only person who's missing. I want to see if Stan Troon's reappeared."

They stood around the car as though it were a gravestone they were paying their respects to. Only the vicar moved, hurrying off to check on his daughter and bring Mrs Paget a cup of tea in a small Thermos.

By now their presence on the green had begun attracting attention from the inhabitants of Lower Gladdock in general. Poole watched David Lake step out of his shop and peer down the street. A number of people had suddenly found an urgent need to walk their dogs on the green. They milled about in groups, gawping at the car and concocting grizzly reasons for its appearance.

"Has someone put it in the local paper or something, sir?" Poole muttered from the side of his mouth as he gazed around at the onlookers.

"That's villages for you, Poole. Everyone knows everyone else's business. Everyone's scrabbling around in the muck of everyone else."

Poole glanced at him. The inspector seemed to lurch between good humour and then these morose spells. He was starting to wonder if they coincided with how they were progressing on the case.

Uniform soon arrived in the form of Davies and Sanders.

"Davies," Poole said, approaching them as they stepped for their car, "I'd like you to make sure all members of the public stay away from the car. The crime scene guys will need the space to get this car out of here and check the area."

"Yes, sir!" Davies said. He turned sharply away and just caught his hat as it slid off to one side.

"Sanders, could you take a statement from Marjory Paget?"

"Yes, sir," Sanita replied. She looked across at the woman who was shakily holding the Thermos and staring intently at the car.

"She's quite upset," Poole said, feeling as though he should say something to warn her. She nodded and moved off.

For some reason, he found himself thinking of his mother.

If she had been able to see him sending the female officer to console the woman while the male one took charge of crowd control, she'd have almost certainly called him part of the fascist state of man, or some such nonsense. The truth was, he had chosen Davies to keep the bystanders back because he thought it was safer than risking him putting his foot in it with Mrs Paget, who looked on the edge as it was.

"Crime scene are here," Brock said, heading towards him. Poole looked over his shoulder and saw Sheila and her van in the distance, giving orders to a couple of white-suited techs. "Let's get going."

"When Stan Troon wasn't here yesterday, it was

possible he'd gone off somewhere, hunting maybe. I mean, a guy who lives in the woods isn't going to be held to routine, is he?" Brock said as they stepped out of the car in the small lay-by that led into the woods.

"And now, sir?" Poole asked they padded along the woodland floor.

"Well, now we have someone else potentially involved in this case missing. More coincidences. I don't like it."

They walked on in silence for a while. The only sound was the crunching underfoot of the carpet of leaves, twigs and needles that made up the floor of the path.

Brock had already told Poole that he wanted to approach quietly, in case Stan Troon decided he didn't want to see them for whatever reason and vanished into the trees. The plan seemed to have worked, as they entered the clearing where the familiar caravan was parked in one corner. Stan Troon looked up at them from its far side, his eyes wide in shock.

"I just found it; I don't..." He turned away from them and back to the object in his hands.

Poole moved quickly, edging towards him and to one side to make sure he could see what he was holding before he got too close.

"Poole!" the inspector hissed from behind him, but Poole ignored it. He had seen what was in Stan's hands.

"Stan, just put the bar down," he said as soon as he recognised the object. It was a crowbar, about three feet in length, bent at one end into a fork and, most notably, covered in blood.

"I just found it here!" Stan shouted, spinning around to them wildly, causing the advance of Brock and Poole to stop with a jolt. "I don't know how it..." He half turned away from them again, looking towards the hedge which ran along the back of his caravan, as though answers were going to jump out at him from there.

"Mr Troon, you need to put the crowbar down," Brock said. Poole glanced at him. His voice sounded calm, but the slightly higher tone left Poole in no doubt that he was stressed.

Stan spun back towards them and seemed to see them properly for the first time, his gaze snapping back and forth between them as though he was centre court at Wimbledon. He was breathing heavily, his eyes wild. Poole tensed himself, ready for Stan Troon to fly at him with the crowbar. He didn't. Instead, he bent slowly, lowering it to the ground and placed it gently on the grass.

Poole moved forward and took his wiry arms, moving them behind his back and cuffing him. As he did so, he felt the tension pour out of him. Brock called across from where he had slumped on the small step at the bottom of the caravan door. "Get crime scene here; they'll need to do a sweep of all this." He waved at the general area. Poole watched him fish a beaten cigarette packet from his jacket pocket as he dialled the station, his heart finally calming from its previous thundering.

He walked Stan Troon to the small bench they had sat on when they had last seen him and rested him on it. "Don't do anything silly like run for it," he said, feeling slightly foolish as he did so. Stan Troon didn't look in any state to be running anywhere. His eyes stared down at the floor in utter confusion.

Poole turned back towards the inspector, who suddenly jumped up from the step and grabbed the front of Poole's jacket in one giant fist.

"Don't you ever take the lead when facing someone who's armed again," he snarled. Smoke billowed from his mouth around Poole's face, whose eyes watered at its impact.

"Yes, sir," he answered, his mouth gaping at this sudden burst of anger.

The inspector breathed heavily, and for a moment Poole thought he might pull back one of those giant fists and strike him. Instead, he pushed Poole away with a growl of frustration and stalked back towards the rear of the caravan.

Poole breathed deeply, his heart pounding now from a new rush of adrenaline. He turned and walked back to Stan Troon, slumped down next to him on the bench and pulled his phone from his pocket.

* * *

The inspector hadn't spoken since they'd left Stan Troon's clearing. He had smoked his cigarette and stared resolutely into the hedgerow until backup had arrived. Poole had then handled the handover and instructions to crime scene before they had both climbed back into the car and headed for the station.

Poole eased the car into space at the station and switched the engine off.

"I'm sorry I snapped," Brock said when the engine had died out, his voice low and even. "But I stand by what I said; you never approach a suspect like that. I'm your superior and I lead on situations like that."

"Yes, sir," Poole answered, his hand still frozen on the door handle.

Brock grunted and opened his door, releasing Poole too.

They walked back towards the station separately, Poole following a few yards behind the inspector. He continued to follow him through the reception, where he ignored Roland's greeting from behind the desk and marched straight through to the canteen.

Poole joined him, unsure of what he was supposed to do next. They made coffee silently next to each other in front of the machine until Brock broke the silence.

"You've looked at a proper picture of Henry Gaven? Like the one in Stan Troon's caravan?"

Poole looked up, confused. "Yes, sir."

"Anything strike you about it?" Brock turned to him with his grey eyes burning.

Poole blinked. "In what way, sir?"

"Right at the start of this when I looked at it. I couldn't help noticing there was a resemblance to some-one. I couldn't place it for a while, but earlier... seeing Stan Troon that upset at finding the crowbar..."

Poole frowned.

"Come on," Brock said, turning away. "I'll show you."

They headed back out to their office, where Brock picked up the file that lay on his desk. He flicked it open and turned two photographs that were laid side by side around for Poole to see. He placed his hands on the desk and leaned over them.

"Oh," he said quietly.

"'Oh' indeed," Brock said. "Bit of a similarity there, isn't there? I was thinking about what Stan had said, that he knew Henry Gaven, but had come to the village four years ago. What if the reason he came to the village was that he had just found out who Henry Gaven was?"

"Found out? You mean because of the accident?"

"Let's go and see, shall we?" Brock said, grinning.

Poole was so relieved to see him in a good mood again he simply nodded and followed him from the room.

The interrogation room was a perfect square. With a cracked, panelled ceiling, sickly yellow strip lights and a small table in the middle of the room, it was suitably grim.

Constable Davies stood in one corner and Stan Troon sat at the table, his thin pale hands wrapped around the cup in front of him as he stared at it. He seemed unaware they had even entered the room until Brock spoke.

"Mr Troon, was Henry Gaven your son?"

Stan's head shot up with a sharp intake of breath as though someone had jabbed him in the ribs. He nodded slowly as his eyes fell back to the cup.

"I didn't know though; didn't know he even existed."

"How did you find out?" Brock continued.

"Someone got in touch with me about the accident. I think it was a mistake, someone who thought I was next of kin or something. They said I was on his birth certificate. By the time I got here he'd already gone away."

"Where were you before?"

"I worked on a fairground. We moved around a lot but we were based in Oxfordshire, not Addervale."

"So you came here looking for Henry," Brock said flatly.

He nodded again.

"And did you try and see Henry in prison?"

"Yeah, I tried. He said he didn't want to see me. I decided to wait until he'd come out and try then."

"And you arranged to stay in the woods until then?"

"Yeah. The vicar's been very kind to me. Even put in a good word for me with Edie."

"And did it work?"

"Sort of." He shrugged. "I used to go over to hers pretty regular. She'd show me pictures of Henry when he was growing up and things." His voice became choked with tears and Davies stepped forward and handed him a pack of tissues from his jacket pocket.

"And what happened when Henry was released from prison?"

"Nothing," he said before blowing his nose loudly. "Edie told me that Henry had sent her a postcard the week before and that he wasn't going to come back. I think that's what made her ill, to be honest."

"And you never saw your son afterwards?"

"No," Stan said, looking up with shimmering eyes. "I never saw him. The vicar said he'd come back eventually, but then Edie got ill and went into the hospital and he still never came back. Then I thought he might turn up at the funeral, but he didn't."

"And did you? I don't remember seeing you there."

"I don't go in for all that church stuff," he said, wiping his eyes. "I paid my respects to Edie in my own way and then waited on the green. When I saw Henry hadn't turned up, I came back here before it all started. Then you two came over. I didn't know that Henry was the one dead then; I just thought you were trying to pin something else on him."

"Something else?" Brock said, his voice suddenly keen. "You think the accident was pinned on him somehow?"

"I don't know. Edie always said he never did it though. She said there must have been some mistake."

"Henry confessed," Brock said firmly.

Stan shrugged. "I only know what Edie told me.

She said he was a good lad and that he never would have drunk and then drove." He looked up at the ceiling. "He never let her visit him in jail either, said it was no place for her to go."

"The crowbar, Mr Troon," Brock said, leaning his large arms on the tabletop. "Was it yours?"

"I—I don't think so." He held his head in his hands as though it was likely to fall off.

"What does that mean?"

"I lost mine a couple of months ago; went to do a job over in Champton and couldn't find it in my stuff. But—the blood." He looked up, his eyes wide and wet. "I didn't kill Henry," he said, his voice choked with emotion. "I don't know how it got blood on it, but it's not his. It can't be." His voice was pleading, desperate.

"Do you know the whereabouts of Malcolm Paget?" Brock threw the question at him as though they had been merely talking about the weather. Poole risked glancing sideways at him. His face was like a wall of granite: set and determined.

"Malcolm? I don't know, why?" Stan's expression moved from one of confusion, thrown by the question, to one of fear. "Has something happened to him?"

"He's currently missing. Maybe it's his blood on the crowbar?"

Stan's eyes darted around the tabletop as though he was following a particularly erratic fly.

"Let me put a little theory to you," Brock said, leaning back and folding his arms. "Henry did come back to the village; he stayed at Edie's."

Stan looked up at him.

"You went there and tried to reconcile with him but he wasn't having it. A fight broke out and you whacked him on the head. You stuck him in a wheelbarrow and pushed him along the footpath to the church. You'd dug the grave the day before; you knew you could dig it a little deeper and then hide the body at the bottom; nobody would ever know. Maybe you thought that was some compensation? Burying him with his gran?"

"No!" Stan shouted, slamming his hands on the tabletop. "I didn't see Henry! I never saw him!"

"And then Malcolm Paget," Brock continued as though he hadn't heard him. "Malcolm told his wife he was going to London, but maybe he came and saw you? Maybe he'd realised who you were and what you'd done?"

"No! No!" Stan cried. He stood now, his fists balled in rage and his eyes bulging. "Henry was my son! I wanted him in my life, not ..." He slumped down again in his chair.

To Poole's surprise, Brock stood up. "Interview terminated at five thirty p.m.," he muttered before leaving the room. Poole followed him.

"What do you think, sir?" he asked as they headed back to their office.

"I think I just pushed a man about the death of his son and I feel like crap about it, that's what I think." Brock marched past the doorway towards their office and headed for the canteen.

"You don't think he killed him?" Poole asked, slightly surprised.

"Do you?" the inspector asked. He took a paper cup from beside the coffee machine and offered Poole one.

Poole thought back to Stan Troon's pained face as they had talked about the death of his son. "He seemed genuine," he said, shrugging. "But the fact he didn't tell us about his relationship with the victim, and now the crowbar..."

"Excuse me, sir."

Poole turned round to see Constable Davies standing, his cheeks flushed.

"Yes, Davies?"

"They've found Malcolm Paget in the woods near Stan Troon's caravan, sir. He's dead."

CHAPTER 13

Poole crunched through the overgrown forest floor with Brock following close behind. He was worried about disturbing evidence, but they didn't have much choice if they wanted to get to the body.

"Another one, eh?" Ronald Smith called to them as they arrived at a small hollow at the bottom of which lay Malcolm Paget.

Brock grunted at him and moved down to the body. Malcolm Paget lay on his side, facing away from the direction Brock and Poole had descended from and towards Ronald Smith, who crouched on the far side in a white crime scene suit.

"Bashed on the head?" Brock said to Ronald, peering closely at the body.

"Yes. And before you ask me, yes, it could have been a crowbar."

Brock sighed, stood up and turned away.

"You seem disappointed?" Ronald said, smiling. "Not fitting with your theory then, eh, Sam? Isn't it annoying when that happens?" He turned to Poole, smirking.

"How long ago do you think he died?" Poole asked, ensuring his face was blank.

The smirk faltered on Ronald's face and he looked back to the body. "Died last night, I'd say," he said. "There's some bruising around his wrists and arms, could be from an altercation before death. I can't tell you much more until we get him back on the table."

Brock grunted and turned away, heading towards where Sheila Hopkins was stood next to a trestle table on which evidence bags were piled.

"Thanks," Poole said to Ronald. He hadn't wanted to, but he couldn't bring himself not to say thank-you to someone who had just given him information.

"Anything, Sheila?" Brock asked as he approached the stout figure in white.

"Not much. We've found the path through the woods where the body was dragged. Came straight from Stan Troon's place."

Brock sighed and ran his hand through his hair as he looked up at the treetops.

"Malcolm Paget wasn't a big man, but it still must have taken some effort to move him," Sheila continued.

Brock's attention snapped back to her. "Two people?"

"I would think so. It's rough ground here. Roots,

sticks and God-knows-what in the way. Getting a body through this would have been a right pain in the arse."

"Thanks, Sheila," Brock said, moving back to the main path and their car.

"I'm going home, Poole. Laura's getting back and I need time to think."

"Yes, sir," Poole said dutifully. Inwardly, he was conflicted. When they were back in the car he began airing his thoughts.

"Sir, who do you think Stan Troon could have got to help him move a body? I mean, I can't think of anyone. He seems like your classic loner to me."

"That's crossed my mind too," Brock said. "The man lives out in the woods on his own. The only person he had any attachment to was Edie Gaven and she's dead. He's done odd jobs for the vicar, I guess, but it's a big ask to move from helping with the church guttering or whatever to asking a man of the cloth to help him get away with murder. No, Stan Troon is not our man, I'm sure of it. Not that that will do much good."

"Sir?" Poole said, glancing at him. The inspector seemed smaller somehow, as though his gigantic frame had shrunk in on itself. He slumped in the passenger seat, looking weary.

"How do you think a jury is going to react when some prosecution lawyer lays out that Stan Troon was an eccentric loner living in the woods who was stalking his son and her grandmother? That he was the one who dug the grave where the body was buried, that it was his crowbar that murdered at least one of the victims, maybe both? Add to all that, we don't have anyone else even on our radar other than David Lake and his henchman. That's where we need to go next. We need to talk to this Hands chap, but tomorrow."

Poole nodded, his focus slipping away from the murder and towards his father. It was time; he had to tell him.

"Sir, there's something I need to tell you."

"That your father is being released from prison tomorrow?" Brock replied immediately.

Poole frowned and for a moment felt silly. He knew the inspector had looked into his background. Why had he assumed that he wouldn't look into his dad's release date?

"Um, yes, sir."

"Do you think he'll try and get in touch?" the inspector asked.

Poole took a deep breath and gripped the wheel tightly. "I have no idea what he'll do."

"Do you want me to put a uniform on your house?"

Poole's thoughts flicked from appreciating the gesture, to imagining Constable Sanders being stationed at his house.

"Thank you, sir, but I'm sure he won't try and contact me. My mum's staying with me."

Brock nodded. "Fine. Well, the offer stands."

They drove on in silence for a few miles, Poole's mind full of images of his father. He had been a fun dad, always ready to play football with him, to listen to stories of his day at school, to read to him when he was in the bath. And then it had all stopped.

For his fifteenth birthday, his parents had bought him a PlayStation 3 to go alongside his already well-used Xbox. His two best friends, Simon and Alfie, had been there, eating cake and playing games while his mother fussed around, bringing an endless supply of food and drink. His dad had been like a kid himself, joking and laughing every time someone lost a life on one of the computer games.

The first real shot hit the TV, exploding it into a million fragments that sprayed across the three teens who were sat cross-legged in front of it. The second hit Poole in the thigh. He screamed out in pain, and then blood from Simon's chest sprayed across him as the third bullet burst through him. Poole had passed out then, with the screams of his mother in his ear and thick blood running down the inside of his jeans.

Over the next few days, he learned that Simon had died. The hole in Poole's leg, operated on twice, was nothing to the hole he felt in his chest. He had learned that his father, also sporting a minor flesh wound to the arm, had been led away by the police after they had found evidence of his criminal empire littered around the house.

By the time he left the hospital, his mum had already put the house on the market and was moving them to start a new life in Oxford, away from the life of false security and happy memories that could never be recreated.

"I didn't know," he said as he pulled the car over into the station car park. Brock turned to him questioningly. "I mean, about my dad. I didn't know what he was. All I knew was that he ran his own business."

"You were just a boy," Brock said softly. "No one should have gone through what you did." He placed a hand on Poole's shoulder. "See you tomorrow, Poole."

Poole nodded in shock and the inspector stepped out of the car, pulled his coat tight around him and headed off towards the town centre.

He even knows about the shooting. The realisation had sent a shudder through him. He had never talked about it with his former colleagues at Oxford, though he guessed they knew. He never wanted to talk about it again.

Poole arrived back at his block of flats and heard whale song as soon as he began ascending the staircase. His heart sank. His mum was here with all her nonsense, but then again, his mum was here. That was what was important.

They just needed to get through tomorrow, and then he would politely send her back to Oxford safe in the knowledge that he was OK.

He opened the door to find his mum lying face down, her lycra-clad bottom pointing to the heavens and a young, swarthy-looking man holding her hips and nodding.

"Yes, Jenny, yes!" the man exclaimed before he seemed to notice Poole and stepped back. "Oh, hello," he said, putting his hands on his hips.

He closed the door as his mum stood up. "Oh, Guy, you're home. I hope you don't mind, but I was just so stressed with everything that's going on, I called Ricardo here to come and realign my core."

"Right," Poole said, giving a curt nod to Ricardo. "I'm actually going out for a bit," he said, surprising himself as much as his mother.

"Oh, right," she said, looking nervous.

"It's fine, Mum," he said. He gave her a smile that he hoped was reassuring and stepped back out of the flat and headed down the stairs.

When he reached the street his first instinct was to head back to the station. It was late now though, and there was nothing that could be done until tomorrow when the inspector was back in.

He looked up and down the street. A few people hurried along in big coats and scarves against the cold. It wasn't a night for being out. Suddenly he thought of the only place he knew other than Sal's, which wouldn't be open: The Mop & Bucket.

He made his way there in a daze, placing one foot after another while his mind flicked between the murders of Henry Gaven and Malcolm Paget, then back to his dad and the death of his friend.

Eventually, he saw the long, low, white building with the faded green sign and stepped inside. He had made his way to the bar and ordered a pint of Bexford

Gold when someone moved alongside him at the bar. He turned to see Sanita Sanders lean against the gleaming mahogany. She turned to him. "Oh, sir!" she said, straightening up.

"Sanders," Poole said awkwardly as the barman approached them. "After you," he said, pointing the barman towards her.

She wore a low-cut cream top and a short denim skirt and, to Poole's mind, looked fantastic, the sudden informality of her clothes intoxicating him and then instantly deflating him. She was probably here on a date, he thought miserably before he began to tune in to her order.

"Two pints of Bexford Gold, one gin and tonic, a merlot and tonic water please."

He breathed a sigh of relief. She must be here with friends, unless her date was a seriously heavy drinker.

The barman sauntered off and she turned back to him. "Do you want to join us, sir? Just a few of us from work having a couple."

"If you're sure?" he said uncertainly. He knew he should say no to this. The last thing they wanted was a superior officer hanging around so they all had to be on their best behaviour. The lure of company, though, and in particular that of Sanita Sanders, was too much.

"Course!" she said, smiling. "The more the merrier. Davies is just filling us in on his love life. It's hysterical." She turned away as a grin broke out across Poole's face, which he tried in vain to subdue. She smiled back at him. "We're over in the far corner," she said, heading off in the direction that he and Brock had sat in previously.

Poole bought a pint of Bexford Gold and ducked through the archway that led into the various nooks and crannies with tables and chairs. He spotted Davies immediately. He was sat under a window that housed an orange table lamp, which gave him an eerie glow. His face itself was bright red, but whether this was from the alcohol or embarrassment, Poole couldn't tell. Sanita caught Poole's eye from a stool on the left of the small group and gestured to an empty one next to her.

"And then there was all this shrieking and commotion," Davies was saying as Poole approached. He was staring soulfully at his beer as though he was reliving a nightmare. The rest of the group were leaning in, hanging on his every word. "And I panicked and was trying to get up, but the baby oil made me slip over and then suddenly the light flicked on and I was lying flat on my back in the middle of the room, naked."

"And what had happened? Why was Lisa shrieking?" asked Roland Hale. Poole thought he looked even larger once he was out from behind the reception desk at Bexford Station.

"That's just it," Davies said miserably. "It wasn't Lisa."

"What?" Hunt said incredulously. "Then who the hell was it?!"

"It was her mum," Davies said quietly.

The whole table erupted in laughter.

"Oh, hello, sir," Davies said, seeing him. Poole was

delighted and surprised to find that the young constable didn't seem remotely embarrassed at his arrival in the middle of this story. Instead, he looked slightly relieved.

Poole was introduced to the still chuckling occupants of the table. As well as Sanita, Davies and Hunt, there was a young, rosy-cheeked woman called Ellie Gould, an administrator in the pathologist's office; and Agatha Jones, an elderly, bird-like woman who was swaying gently on her stool. As he took his seat the group all looked at him expectantly.

"I'm sorry, Davies," Poole said, looking across the table at him, "but I'm going to have to know the beginning of that story."

Davies hung his head and groaned as everyone else around the table laughed and Roland began shouting, "Again! Again!" and hitting the table.

BROCK WALKED the short distance from the station to his house at varying speeds. At times his powerful legs ate up the distance, as he thought of Laura's soft smile and eyes, alive with mischief and warmth, then slowing as he imagined that soft, kind face in tears. Hearing that her dream might be further away than ever, and worse, that he had been lying to her.

Eventually, he arrived at the small row of neat houses that formed Cedar Avenue and walked down the path. He took a deep breath and opened the door.

"Hello?" he shouted down the hallway as he hung his coat up.

"Hello!" Laura's voice shouted back. She appeared from the kitchen doorway carrying two glasses of red wine.

"Wine?" Brock said, smiling.

She wrapped her arms around him and kissed him lightly. "I read a magazine article on the plane that sometimes couples can put so much pressure on themselves that the stress can slow the whole thing happening in the first place."

"Oh, right," he said, smiling. Something dark squirmed in his gut.

"I thought we'd get a takeaway tonight; I'm shattered," she said, turning back towards the kitchen.

He followed her through and they both sat at the breakfast bar.

"So come on, tell me what he's like," she said eagerly.

"Well, he looks like he's made out of pipe cleaners for a start—all limbs."

"Right ..." Laura said slowly.

"And his hair looks like it's something that grows under a tree."

"Oh, for goodness sake, Sam, what's he like?!"

Brock sighed and looked down at his glass. "His whole life has been defined by something that happened to him as a kid. I don't think he's made a single decision in his life since that wasn't determined by it."

"Bloody hell. The lad sounds a wreck," Laura said, her face full of sympathy.

"Actually, he's not. He's going to be a bloody good detective, and he's all right company."

Laura smiled and punched him on the arm. "And there was me worrying you were going to go all crazy that he was going to die at any moment! Instead, you've gone and made a friend!" She laughed and took another sip of wine.

Brock smiled, but she saw that somehow it didn't reach his eyes.

"Oh," she said, putting her hand on his arm.

Brock took a large swig of wine before talking. "There was a suspect," he said. "He was holding a crowbar and Poole ran towards him and I ..." He placed the glass down on the countertop. "I froze."

She put her glass down and stepped off her stool, throwing her arms around his neck.

"Oh, Sam, you don't need to feel bad about that after what you've been through."

"I don't feel bad about it, I feel bloody foolish. Thank goodness he didn't realise, but I was bloody angry with him afterwards as well."

"I'm sure he understood."

"It's not that."

"Then what is it?" Laura asked.

"With all that happened to him, all he's been through. He ran towards the danger."

CHAPTER 14

"They've matched DNA from both Henry Gaven and Malcolm Paget on the crowbar," Brock said, putting his phone back into his pocket. It had rung almost as soon as Poole had picked the inspector up from the station car park and so, as yet, they had not had time to talk.

"It's not looking good for Stan Troon, is it, sir?" Poole said.

"No it's not, but a case is never closed until you've followed all the leads to the end."

Poole nodded and pulled into the car park of the Little Chef where they were to meet David Lake's right-hand man, Hands. Lake had called into the station asking for Brock early that morning. He'd told him that he'd been thinking of what the inspector had said and had spoken to Hands again. Apparently, he had some more information for them, and knowing that they would want to speak to him anyway, Lake had arranged a meeting.

They stepped out of the car and headed towards the small café, the cars roaring along the main road behind them.

They spotted Hands as soon as they had entered. A large, hulking man was squashed into a booth against the far wall. His slitted eyes darted across to them and he nodded in a jerky motion that sent his multiple chins wobbling impressively. They sat on the bench opposite him, Poole pulling his notepad and pen out, which Hands eyed suspiciously.

"So," Brock said. "You're our mysterious walker from the footpath in Lower Gladdock?"

Hands grinned. "That were me!"

"So come on, tell me what you saw."

"I saw Gaven in the lane and told David," he said in a breathless, wheezy voice. "I followed him back to the village and saw him arguing with that weird couple."

"The Pagets," Brock said.

Hands nodded. "That's who David said they were, yeah."

"And then what?"

"I followed him back towards the lane, but there was a bit I didn't mention before." He looked slightly sheepish. "I didn't think anything of it." He shrugged.

"Well?" Brock demanded.

"He met someone on the grass bit as he was going back."

"The village green?" Poole asked.

"Yeah." Hands looked at him with a smile, apparently finding the phrase "village green" amusing.

"Who did he meet?" Brock asked, his voice tense.

"Some girl. Had mad hair all over the place. Looked like a loony to me..."

"What colour was her hair?"

Hands frowned. "Brown?" he said, his sweating brow wrinkling.

"And were they arguing? Talking? What?"

"Well she was hugging him and she said something, but he just pushed her away and walked off."

"And what did she do?"

"Nothing. Just went running off. So I didn't think much of it."

"And then? What happened to Henry Gaven?"

"And then nothing. He just went back to his gran's place. Next thing I hear is he's turned up dead." He paused and looked at them both. "But I didn't do him in, and neither did David."

Brock leaned back in his seat and stared at the Hands as though deciding something. "Give Poole your contact details; address and phone number," he said before standing and heading back out to the car park.

Poole joined him there a few moments later having got the information, to find him smoking.

"Three months I hadn't had a cigarette for, three bloody months. Now I'm back on it and my little swimmers are probably keeling over in coughing fits."

Poole began to laugh and then stifled it as he saw the inspector's expression.

"That's what this bloody case is doing to me," Brock continued. He moved off towards the car suddenly and Poole jogged to keep up with his long stride.

"He was obviously talking about Sandra Hooke," he said as he moved alongside. "I take it we're going to see her?"

"Bloody right we are," Brock answered. "I don't care how fragile she is, she needs to start answering some questions. Like why she hasn't mentioned that she saw Henry Gaven on the night he died."

Brock climbed in the car, cigarette still in hand. Poole climbed in next to him and discreetly lowered the passenger window from the controls on his door.

"There's something not right here, Poole," Brock said, turning and blowing a long jet of smoke through the crack. "Not right at all."

"It doesn't look as though the vicar is here," Poole said as they walked towards the door of the vicarage. He gestured to the empty driveway on which Nathaniel Hooke's car normally stood.

Poole pressed the Victorian doorbell and waited only a few moments before the door was opened by Sandra Hooke. Her eyes widened as she looked at the two of them, but she silently turned and walked back into the house, leaving the door open for them to enter through.

They followed her into the front room where she sat down, perched on the edge of the sofa and waited. She had a kind of smile on her face that Poole couldn't decide was one of serenity or detachment.

"Sandra, we need to ask you some more questions about Henry Gaven," Brock said, taking the same seat as he had done on their last visit.

"I knew you would," she said softly. "Policemen always want to know everything."

Poole frowned slightly at her flat, calm tone. She seemed to be a very different woman today. Less manic, less scared.

"Did you talk to him after he had been released from prison?" Brock continued.

"No," Sandra said, smiling.

Brock paused for a moment before continuing. "We have a witness that says you spoke to him on the village green, late on Friday night. The night he was killed."

"Henry was brave," she said, tilting her head to one side. "Not like Charlie. Charlie wasn't brave. He was afraid of things."

Brock said nothing. Poole turned to him but Brock lifted his hand slightly from his knee, telling him to say nothing. Her head straightened up and she stared at a point behind them, as though they weren't there at all.

"Charlie killed himself and then Charlotte killed herself and then Henry died because he might have killed himself."

Poole noted this down, but he had no idea why. This was gibberish. The woman was clearly unwell.

"Did you kill Charlie Lake, Sandra?"

Her gaze snapped back into the room and to Brock. "Didn't you hear me?" she giggled. "Charlie killed himself."

"Sandra, don't say another word!" a voice boomed from the doorway which led out into the hall. Nathaniel Hooke marched in and stood between the two men and his daughter. "You have no right, Inspector! No right to enter my home and start questioning my daughter and confusing her!"

"I have every right," Brock answered, standing up. Despite the vicar's tall frame, the inspector towered over him. "This is a murder enquiry and I believe your daughter has been withholding evidence."

"She's not well!" the vicar cried in a whine, throwing his hands in the air. "Can't you see?!"

"Then she can come into the station and be seen by specialists who will make sure that any interview with her does not upset her."

"No!" cried the vicar again. "If that's what you want, then you must go through the proper channels and have a warrant for her arrest or whatever it is you need."

"Arrest?" Brock said quietly, leaning towards the vicar slightly. "Now why would you think we'd want to arrest her?"

The vicar narrowed his eyes and breathed in slowly

through his nose. "I would like you both to leave now," he said, his voice quivering slightly.

Brock nodded and headed out towards the hallway with Poole following. As he left, he glanced at Sandra, who still sat on the sofa. The glazed smile she had worn since they had arrived was still there as her eyes caught his. He felt a chill run down the back of his spine, just as he had the first time he had seen her, leaning over the grave of Edie Gaven and peering down at her father.

CHAPTER 15

"Do you think he's protecting her, sir?" Poole said when they were back in the car, heading towards Bexford Station. Poole flicked on the wipers as the darkening sky finally gave way to rain.

"Of course he is," Brock answered. "What we don't know is to what extent."

"Sir?"

"Is he a man protecting his troubled daughter from further upset and trauma by shielding her from our questions and reliving what happened, or is he shielding her because he knows or at least suspects she might have been responsible?"

Poole thought about Sandra Hooke, how small and frail she had seemed when he had first seen her. Then he pictured those eyes, dilated and wild.

"I could see her doing it," he said quietly.

"Me too," Brock replied. "Try and find out what

doctor she's seeing, see what kind of medication she's on."

"We could bring her in."

"We could, but I don't see what good it would do. We haven't got any evidence linking her to the murder other than some criminal saying he saw her talk to the victim on the night he died. Any confession we might get out of her would be chalked up to whatever the hell is wrong with her, and I don't want to go down that road without hard evidence to back it up."

"So what now?" Poole asked.

"Now? Now we have lunch with my wife."

"We, sir?"

"She wants to meet you."

"That's nice, sir, but I'd like to check on my mum if that's OK?"

Brock turned to him. "Your father gets out today," he said flatly. "Have you heard from him?"

"No," Poole said, trying to keep the tension out of his voice. "I'm not expecting to; I just want to make sure Mum is OK."

"Of course. Well let's pick her up and she can come with us, eh?"

"Oh, right. Thank you, sir."

Poole gave a weak smile to his superior, who turned back to stare out of the window. He wasn't entirely sure how he felt about introducing the inspector to his mother. The inspector's gruff no-nonsense attitude to pretty much everything didn't seem to align with his mother's alternative views on things.

A few minutes later they had pulled up outside the flat and Poole had jogged up the steps.

"Mum?" he called out as he opened the door.

"Guy? What are you doing back?" She emerged from the kitchen wearing an apron.

Poole took a deep breath and leaned against the door frame. "Do you want to come for lunch and meet my new boss and his wife?"

"Oh, Guy! I'd love to! Let me just turn the oven off again. I was just baking you some of my flapjacks."

Poole winced. His mother's flapjacks consisted of porridge oats stuck together with mashed banana. They were healthy and disgusting.

She took the apron off and walked across to him, placing a hand on each shoulder.

"Have you heard anything?"

"No," he said. He stepped forward and hugged her. He knew why she was being more batty than usual; she was scared.

"Come on," he said, releasing her. "Let's go."

They headed down to the car, Brock climbing out as they approached.

"Mrs Poole, very nice to meet you," he said, extending his hand.

"Oh no, the pleasure is all mine!" she answered, pushing his hand to one side and embracing him. "And please," she said into his ear. "Call me Jenny."

"Er, right," Brock answered, looking at Poole with an expression that was half confused and half pleading for help.

"Come on then," Poole said, putting his hand on his mother's back until she got the hint and let go.

"And what's your name, Inspector?" Jenny continued when they got in the car.

"Sam."

"Oh, lovely. A good strong name."

"Thank you," Brock answered. Poole glanced across and noticed a smirk on his face.

He directed Poole to a small car park on one side of the main town square.

"Oh Guy, it's such a beautiful town," Jenny said, spinning around.

They headed across to a small, pretty café with Brock grumbling. "Small portions, big price. Bloody rip-off, this place, but it's in the town square so they just keep sucking them in."

"It's corporate greed and nothing more," Jenny chimed in.

"Exactly!" Brock said, nodding at her and opening the door.

They found Laura Brock at a corner table, a latte in front of her.

"Hello!" she said, rising as they approached. Brock made the introductions before heading to the counter with Poole to order more drinks, leaving Jenny hugging Laura.

"This case, Poole," he said once they had ordered four cheese toasties and three more lattes. "It's bothering me. All of this pointing towards Stan Troon—someone's done that deliberately. Someone's set him up. Now I can't help but think Sandra Hooke is something to do with it, but could she have planned to set someone up that meticulously? She doesn't seem in the right mind to do something like that."

Poole's phone buzzed in his pocket. He pulled it out and stared at the screen. He didn't recognise the number.

"Hello?" he said, putting it to his ear.

"Hello, son."

Poole swayed backwards and reached out to the counter to steady himself. His chest felt as though it was going to explode.

"Poole?" Brock said, turning to him.

"Aren't you going to say hello, then?" the voice on the phone said. It was familiar to Poole, but at the same time alien, like a voice he'd remembered from a film he'd watched rather than that of his father.

"What do you want?" he said, his voice sounding in his ears as though someone else had been talking.

"Well, what do you think I want?" the voice replied, laughing. "I want to catch up! See how you're doing? Is the new place working out?"

Poole reeled. He felt like he might be sick.

Brock took the phone from his unresisting hand and hung up the call.

"Was that him?" he said, passing the phone back.

Poole nodded.

"Come on," he said in an abrupt voice. He turned back towards the table and Poole followed in a daze.

"I'm sorry, Laura, but we're getting this to go and heading back to the station."

"What's happened?" she asked, her face paling as she stood.

Brock turned to Jenny. "I'm afraid your husband has just called your son."

"Oh God!" Jenny said, standing up so suddenly her chair went flying backwards, crashing loudly against the flagstones of the floor.

Jenny picked it up as Brock marched back to the counter and asked for their food to be wrapped to go.

"Go and get in the car," he said to Poole, who came up next to him with his arm around his mother. Poole nodded and headed out.

"Are they in danger?" Laura said when they had gone.

"I don't know," Brock answered, his large brow knotted in a frown. "But I'm going to keep them at the station until I know where this guy is and what he wants."

The woman behind the counter handed over their food in a brown paper bag and they paid and moved to the door.

"I'll see you later," Brock said, kissing his wife lightly on the cheek and turning away towards the car. She caught his arm and pulled him back towards her. She kissed him hard on the lips.

"You're going to make a great dad, you know. Just be careful, will you?"

Brock felt something inside him crumble.

"There's something I need to tell you," he said, his eyes feeling out the floor. "The test I had, you know, to check everything was OK—well, it wasn't."

"What do you mean?"

"Apparently I have slow swimmers," he said, looking up at her, his grey eyes glistening.

"That was months ago," she said, her voice sounding hollow. "You've known all this time?"

He nodded, his heart wrenching.

She sighed and grabbed the lapels of his coat. "Sam Brock, you are a bloody idiot."

"I know." He reached a hand up and pushed a stray hair from her face back behind her ear.

"I know you," she continued. "And I know this will have been eating you up. You should have told me."

He nodded again.

"But we'll deal with this; we'll work it out." She stood on tiptoes and kissed him on the forehead. "Now go and sort this out."

He squeezed her hand, smiled and turned back to the car.

They drove back to the station in silence, Poole's face set in a grim expression as he drove the car in a slow and steady manner.

When they'd parked and stepped out of the car, Brock pulled him aside.

"Take your mum into the canteen and get her

settled, then get on to Sandra Hooke's doctor. I'm going to go and bring her in. I don't think it will work, but we've got to do something to stir the pot."

"Yes, sir," Poole said. He moved to turn away and then hesitated. "Thank you, sir."

Brock grunted and gestured for them to get on with it. The three of them headed towards the station, Poole propping up his mother, whose pale face stared blankly, unseeing, in front of her.

Once Poole and his mother had safely been delivered into the canteen, Brock stepped back into the main office and looked around the largely empty desks.

"Davies," Brock called across the office once they were inside. "I want you to come with me."

"Yes, sir!" Davies said, jumping up from his desk and spilling a cup of coffee across his desk. Brock closed his eyes and muttered under his breath as Davies mopped up the spillage with a serviette.

POOLE SAT STARING at the wall, his mother's hand held in his.

They had exchanged few words; there wasn't much to say. Their worst fears were being realised. His father had been released from prison, and his first act had been to find them, to contact them.

How on earth had he gotten Poole's number? How had he known about the move to Bexford? Poole's thoughts drifted to the consequences of this news. Would he have to move again? To leave the country?

He looked up as movement caught his eye and saw Sanita Sanders entering the room. He realised suddenly what he needed; a distraction. He needed to focus on the case.

"Mum, are you OK here for a bit?" He turned to look at her. She nodded, forcing a nervous smile. He squeezed her hand and left her, making his way to Sanita.

"Hi," he said as he reached her at the coffee machine.

"Hey. How're you?"

"Fine. Do you think you could give me a hand for a bit?"

She smiled at him and, despite the circumstances, he felt his stomach flip.

"Course. What are we doing?"

"Trying to find a doctor," he answered, smiling back at her.

CHAPTER 16

Brock and Davies arrived at Lower Gladdock in torrential rain.

"Park on the green," Brock said, pointing out into the gloom.

"Yes, sir," Davies said. He gripped the steering wheel and steered it to the right.

He was trying to play it cool, but he hadn't had this much adrenaline coursing through him since he had attempted to reverse park in front of some builders.

Not only had the inspector asked him to take him to the village, he had asked him to drive as fast as he could. Davies had gone for it, showing off all of the new skills he had learned on his recent advanced driving course. He had nailed it, the perfect high-speed bit of driving. Now his blood was pumping and he was ready for anything.

The car hit the curb hard, jolting him out of his seat. The sound of the inspector's head hitting the ceiling rang out above the rain. He turned to Davies, leaned across him and turned the engine off.

"Thank you, Davies," he said in a flat tone. "Come on." He climbed out of the car and ran towards the vicarage. Davies followed in a loping run, hitting most of the puddles that Brock seemed to avoid.

By the time they arrived at the vicarage they were both soaked through. Brock pressed the bell as they both squared under the small overhang that stood above the door.

The door opened to reveal Nathaniel Hooke. He stared down his long nose at them.

"Yes, Inspector?"

"I'm afraid, Vicar, that we are here to take Sandra in for formal questioning."

"I'm afraid it's not a good time," the vicar replied. He stepped back and began to close the door, but Brock shot out an enormous foot and jammed it open.

"This isn't optional," Brock said, pushing forward hard at the door. The vicar stumbled backwards and began edging down the hall.

Brock then heard Sandra's voice from upstairs. She wailed with a noise like a wounded horse, insensible. He moved to the base of the staircase and stared upwards. He pulled his phone from his pocket and called Poole.

SANITA SLAMMED the phone down in frustration.

"Still nothing?" Poole asked as he stood up.

"No. Either Sandra Hooke goes to a doctor that's absolutely miles away, maybe not even Addervale, or she doesn't go to one."

Poole's jaw tensed as he put his coat on. "My guess is on the latter. I'm going to get over to the village, see what Brock and Davies are up to. Thanks for your help."

She smiled and followed him out of the small office and back into the open-plan section of the building.

Poole's phone buzzed in his pocket as he headed towards reception. He looked at the screen. Brock.

"Sir?"

"Get over here now, and bring ..."

There was a pause before a loud bang and the line went dead.

He felt his stomach drop. He reached out one hand to the wall to steady himself and turned around.

"Sanders! Get backup to Lower Gladdock now!", he heard a voice scream, and as he turned and ran through reception towards his car, he realised it had been his.

POOLE SPED down the narrow country lanes at a speed he knew was reckless in this weather. The driving rain had turned the tarmac into sheets of glistening water that shone in his headlights as he tore along them.

The inspector's voice had been urgent and

demanding, and adrenaline had been pouring through Poole's body since the line had gone.

He didn't know what the inspector had uncovered or gotten into, but he knew that it would lead them to the killer of Henry Gaven and Malcolm Paget. He just hoped the inspector's name wouldn't be added to that list.

He sped past the sign welcoming him to Lower Gladdock and soon entered the road that swept around the edge of the village green. He screeched to a halt, realising with a jolt of panic that he had no idea where the inspector had gone. Poole stepped out of the car, the driving rain stinging against his cheeks, and looked around wildly.

An arm snaked around his neck suddenly from behind and a long, sharp kitchen knife danced in front of his vision.

"Please, don't move," a voice said in his ear.

BROCK OPENED his eyes and saw blood. He knew it was his own because the throbbing at the back of his head was so intense it was blurring his vision.

He pushed himself up to his knees slowly, breathing hard. There was a significant pool of blood on the floor in front of him. He tried to ignore it and stand. He swayed slightly and held onto the wall for support.

There was a roll of thunder in the distance as he

turned slowly around, looking for signs of his attacker. There was no sign of anyone, and Sandra's moans from upstairs were now silent.

He realised that Davies lay in front of him on his chest, his face turned away from him. He dropped to his knees heavily next to him and turned him over slowly. No blood and he was breathing. He placed him in the recovery position and looked around for his phone, but couldn't see it.

Behind him, the front door was open. He stumbled towards it, stepping out into the black, wet night. There was no one in the driveway. He made his way to the road and looked up and down. Nothing.

Then he noticed the lights were on in the church and something clicked in his mind. The old building had been dark when he had arrived.

CHAPTER 17

Brock could hear the screaming before he'd even reached the thick wooden door that stood open at the front of the church. It echoed out from the entrance hall, reverberating around the ancient stone and defying even the weather to drown it out. He ran through the short stone porch and inside.

Nathaniel and Sandra Hooke were behind the altar, which stood on a small raised platform at the far end of the church. Poole stood in front of the vicar. The light from the large candle burning at the centre of the altar glinted off a large knife that was held at his throat.

Brock's stomach lurched as the words "The Cursed Detective" flashed in his brain. It was happening again. He was going to lose another partner, and this one after only a few days.

Sandra's screams died out, the echoes of them

fading as she leaned across the ornate tablecloth which draped over the altar and sobbed.

Nathaniel Hooke's eyes were wide, dancing around the church, glinting in the candlelight.

"Nathaniel," Brock said, moving slowly up the aisle. "I know you were trying to protect your daughter." His voice boomed around the space. He paused and leaned against a wooden pew. His brain was working furiously despite the head wound. He'd had it all wrong. Yes, this was related to the accident all those years ago, but it wasn't about revenge, it was about a cover-up.

"Was it you driving the car the night Charlie was killed, Sandra?"

The young woman looked up suddenly, her face taut and pale.

"She was so young," the vicar said quietly. He reached his hand down and stroked the back of his daughter's head. Brock noticed she flinched slightly at his touch.

The inspector inched along the aisle towards them.

"She was driving that night four years ago, wasn't she?" he said, directing his question at the vicar again. "It was Sandra who was over the limit and who knocked Charlie Lake down."

The vicar nodded, tears rolling down his pale, drawn face.

"Only it wasn't just an accident, was it? You found out that she'd arranged to meet Charlie there somehow, called him maybe? That's why he didn't have the

Lakes' family dog with him; that's why he was out at three in the morning on the village green."

Brock took another step closer.

"You knew how to protect her though, didn't you? All you had to do was to get Henry to say he'd been driving. He was in the car too. It was easy. The church already owned Edie Gaven's cottage and she was ill. You promised to look after Edie for Henry, didn't you? Promised you would pay for her to get the care she needed at home and that they would both be looked after once he was released. You even worked on his behalf to get him released early."

He took another small step as a crack of thunder rumbled overhead.

"That was part of the plan though, wasn't it? You wanted Henry to confess so that there was no suspicion on Sandra, but you knew you still needed to clean house, didn't you?" Brock edged closer to the platform.

"The Pagets came to you because they were worried about their daughter. You kindly offered to go down to London and see if you could help. You got her into a drug rehabilitation program there which you conveniently began to volunteer at."

The inspector was winging it now, his mouth working before his brain could keep up with it. He had to keep talking, keep distracting until he could get close enough.

"Charlotte seemed to be doing well. Was that when she started talking about confessing that she was in the car that night too? Was that when you decided she had to go as well? I'm not sure how you managed to get your hands on the drugs, but I imagine you left some at her bedsit to tempt her. Maybe after making her go over the accident to ensure she would be at a low ebb? Either way, I think you then went back and gave her a second dose, right after the first. The pathologist said there had been no new needle tracks for months, then suddenly two at once."

Brock moved forward again and the vicar's head jerked up towards him from his daughter. He froze and continued talking.

"And then Henry Gaven was due to be released. And so you had to deal with the real problem. You knew that once he got out he'd start putting two and two together about Charlotte's death, and then what? He'd be after you for more money, that's what."

Brock shuffled his feet a little farther forward, almost imperceptibly.

"I think Henry was on to you straight away. I think he even suspected you of doing away with poor Edie. I mean, the timing was very convenient wasn't it? Her getting ill just before he was going to be released and then dying before he could even see her? Then I guess he'd had a drink, probably upset about his gran, and went to the Pagets'. Did he tell them that there was something suspicious about the death of Charlotte? That they should look into it? He obviously didn't tell them about you, did he? Maybe he was still planning to extort you for one last pay-off first? But you didn't know that at the time, did you? Not until later. Henry met

Sandra on the way back to Edie's house. I guess that she came home and told you she had seen him. You went straight to Edie's house and smashed him over the head. I'm not sure how you lured him into the shed. Maybe he was already there, getting logs for the fire or something? Of course, the really clever part was how you had set up Stan Troon to take the fall.

"Do you know? It was bothering me how perfect a fall guy Stan was. I mean, how could someone have arranged for him to be there when another prime suspect was needed?

"I bet you couldn't believe your luck when he showed up four years ago. A ready-made patsy to take the fall whenever you were ready. You had let him stay in the woods, which the church also owns, and you'd taken his crowbar as soon as you'd known when Henry would be released. It was clever you telling us that Stan had supposed to be working for you that day we went looking for him. It made us suspect him straight away."

The vicar's attention had turned back to Sandra, who had raised her head. She was staring at Brock now, her eyes wide. The tears had gone and had been replaced by an intense gaze that looked to Brock like blind fury.

"Malcolm Paget found out something about his daughter's death in London. I don't know what. We probably never will. Maybe he spoke to people in her rehab group and they all told him the same thing, that she was well on the road to recovery and they had never seen it coming. You'd told him a different story though, hadn't you? That you had visited her not long before, and she had seemed very down and that you were worried? Is that what he came to ask you about? Why those two stories didn't match? Luckily for you, you still had Stan's crowbar hidden."

Brock's eyes looked into Sandra's.

"Did he make you help him move Malcolm's body into the woods, Sandra?" Brock said.

The small frame of Sandra Hooke started to rock slightly as she took faster breaths.

"Leaving the crowbar at Stan's was easy enough; he would take the fall for everything. And most importantly of all, Sandra would be safe."

"Sandra is unwell!" Nathaniel screamed desperately. The sudden noise above the dull roar of the storm made Poole jump.

"Sandra," Brock said. He began walking forward, his eyes fixed on hers now. "What happened when you drove back from Bexford that night? Was it a joke gone wrong? You told us that Charlie had killed himself. What was it? A game? Were you playing chicken and he didn't move?"

Sandra looked wildly at her father and then back to Brock.

"I think after your mother died, your dad couldn't bear the thought of losing you as well. So he covered your tracks. But what's he been doing to you, Sandra? He's been virtually keeping you prisoner."

She turned and stared at her father again.

Sandra screamed—a bloodcurdling, primal noise of

bitter anguish. She grabbed the large candlestick from the altar, pushed past her father and ran towards a side door in the church. Nathaniel Hooke tore after her, dragging Poole with him. Brock broke into a run but slowed as his head throbbed and his vision swayed. He staggered on through the small passage leading out into the graveyard.

As he stepped out into the thunderous night, a flash of lightning lit up the sky and illuminated the three figures to his left.

Nathaniel Hooke stood with his left arm still around Poole's neck, his right still held the knife to his throat. Sandra stood next to him, her eyes glazed over, staring into the rain with the candlestick hanging limply at her side.

Brock moved closer until he was just a few feet away, his hands raised in front of him.

"It's all over now, Nathaniel. We can look after Sandra, get her the help that she needs."

An explosion of thunder rolled above their heads.

"I won't let her go!" screamed the vicar, his eyes bulging. "I won't," he said in a wail. He shook his head vigorously, making the rain fly off his limp hair in all directions, as though he was trying to free something from his head. Sandra was still motionless, like a robot that had been switched off.

"Let Sandra and the sergeant come to me and we can look after her. We can make her better," Brock shouted above the roar of the rain.

There was another flash and a deafening crack

sounded from the tower of the church as the lightning bolt struck the corner of the old stone, which exploded above their heads.

Brock dived to his right, landing in the wet grass and rolling as the sound of stone crashing on the path behind him rang in his ears. He opened his eyes as thunder rolled across the sky above him. He turned towards where the others had been. Only Sandra still stood.

He climbed to his feet and ran towards Poole, who was slowly getting to his feet.

"You OK, Poole?" he shouted as he came alongside the rising figure.

"Yes," Poole said, his voice small. Brock followed his gaze down to the vicar, who lay awkwardly, his head on one side, eyes staring sightlessly. A pool of blood spread around his head like a halo.

Brock bent down and felt the man's wrist, looked up at Poole and shook his head.

There was a clatter as Sandra dropped the candlestick on the stone path.

The inspector leaned across and picked it up before taking the knife that lay next to the vicar's lifeless hand.

He stood and looked at Sandra Hooke. Her eyes were vacant again, staring out into the rain as though she didn't even notice it. He looked at Poole, who stood, staring at the vicar's body as the sound of sirens approaching rose louder through the storm.

CHAPTER 18

"Pretty impressive back there in the church," Poole said to Brock, who was sat on the edge of a hospital bed with a thunderous look in his eye.

"I was trying to get him to confess," Brock said with a grunt. "I knew we didn't have anything on him, not really. I needed him to admit it and hope that Sandra would be able to back it up, though Lord knows what state she's going to be in after all that." His face hardened. "Remember what I kept saying about this case, Poole? Too many coincidences. I realised it when I walked into that church. There were too many things linking the vicar to all the victims. Not Sandra, mind you—the vicar."

Poole nodded. "Apparently the doctor who's checked over Sandra says she's definitely been drugged. They're running tests on her now."

Brock shook his head. "I'd wondered about how

much the accident had affected Sandra and Charlotte for that matter. Losing a friend would be traumatic, awful, but young people are resilient. I wondered if there was something else going on there and there was guilt. They had all been in the car that night, all except Charlie Lake that is." He shook his head again sorrowfully. "Such a bloody waste. All those young lives lost or wasted. And now Sandra Hooke is going to do time for helping her father."

"She still drove that car four years ago; she still killed Charlie Lake," Poole reminded him.

"I think so, yes, but we don't have any proof she did. Do you remember what she said the first time we talked to her at the vicarage?"

Poole shrugged and shook his head.

"She'd said how it was just a joke," Brock continued. "That she was just having fun. That's why I asked her if it had been a game that had gone wrong. I think they were drunk and messing around that night and decided to play a joke on Charlie and it went wrong. I think she was still stuck in that night four years ago."

He paused and looked up at Poole. "And you're sure Davies is all right?"

"Yes, sir. I made him go home and rest," Poole said, grinning. Brock had already asked twice if Constable Davies was okay, and said that he shouldn't have left him back at the vicarage three times. Poole had explained that Davies had been completely fine, with just a minor bump on the head to show for his night's work.

The door of the room opened and Laura Brock rushed in, her eyes full of tears.

"Oh my God, Sam, are you OK?!" she said, throwing her arms around the inspector's huge frame.

"I'm fine. It's just a scratch. They just wanted to check me out before they let me go." He made eyes at Poole over her shoulder, which suggested he should not mention the doctor's recommendation that he should stay in overnight.

"Are you OK?" she said, turning to Poole.

"Yes thank you, Mrs Brock."

"Oh please, Laura," she said, laughing. "Saying 'Mrs Brock' reminds me of my mother-in-law, and, believe me, that's not a good thing.

Brock laughed loudly and stood up from the bed. The change in the inspector was instantaneous. As soon as his wife had entered the room he had brightened somehow, the pain from his head wound and the stress of the last few hours melting away into a smile.

"Well, Sam's a bloody nightmare on detail so you're going to have to help fill me in on what on earth happened tonight."

Poole turned to Brock, who smiled, hunched his shoulders and turned his palms upwards. "Hey, the lady gets what the lady wants," he said, laughing.

Poole explained the confrontation with Nathaniel Hooke, watching Laura Brock's face contort through concern and surprise as he did so. He paused as he reached the part where lightning had struck the church.

"So did Sandra hit her father with the candlestick? Or was it falling masonry?" Her eyes darted between them as they, in turn, looked at each other.

"We don't know yet," Brock answered. "Neither of us saw, but forensics will soon know."

"That poor woman," Laura said sadly. She moved back to the inspector and squeezed him around the shoulders. "What will happen to her now?"

"She might get away with self-defence in the case of her father, but we need to find out the real story about the accident that killed Charlie Lake. She's not innocent in this, Laura," Brock said.

"I know, but if she was on drugs? She might not have known what she was doing."

The inspector frowned, his gaze turning towards the ceiling. "Poole," he said suddenly, returning his eye to him. "Do you remember the vicar mentioned making Sandra some sort of special herbal tea to help her relax?"

"Yes," Poole said gravely, realising what the inspector was getting at.

Brock nodded. "I think it would be a good idea to see what was in that tea."

The door opened and the doctor arrived. Poole watched with amusement as Brock took turns in trying to bat away the concerns of both his doctor and his wife. Eventually, he seemed to win, and the doctor agreed that he could be discharged under the supervision of Laura.

They stepped out into night air, which still had the

crackle of electricity in it despite the passing of the storm.

"Can we give you a lift anywhere, Guy?" Laura offered. She clung to Brock as though he might fly away in the light breeze, her arms wrapped around his waist.

"Yes, we can," Brock jumped in before he could answer. "I had a uniformed officer take Poole's mum back to his flat earlier, but I'll get them to meet us at The Mop & Bucket for a stiff drink."

"Oh, Sam, come on. You might have concussion!"

"A couple of pints isn't going to make much difference, is it?" he said, back to the gruff manner Poole had come to expect. "And anyway, it's tradition. We've closed a case, we go to the pub."

Laura stepped away and raised her eyebrows at him, arms folded.

"We'll get back to the whole ovulation chart mumbo-jumbo from tomorrow," the inspector said irritably.

Laura punched him on the arm playfully and took Poole's arm instead.

"Come on then, Guy, you can tell me about yourself while this idiot destroys his brain cells and his sperm count in one fell swoop."

Poole laughed and then stopped himself as he caught the inspector's expression.

"So come on then, how are you finding Bexford?" Laura asked as they headed down the streetlamp-lit pavement.

"I like it," Poole replied. "The inspector took me to

Sal's and The Mop & Bucket and they were both amazing."

Laura stopped and turned to her husband.

"Thanks a lot, Poole. The soul of bloody discretion you are," Brock said, rolling his eyes.

"Sorry, sir. I..." Poole stopped, his eyes drifting beyond the inspector to the figure that was walking towards them.

It was a man, his coat collar lifted up on his long coat, a crop of short white hair on his head and a cigar hanging from one corner of his mouth.

"Poole?" Brock said, noting his expression and turning to the man.

"Aren't you going to introduce me, Guy?" the man said, grinning. He turned to him, looking him up and down. "It's good to see you, son."

POOLE FELT a blow that was almost physical at the sight of his father. It had been ten years since he had last seen him, ten years of wondering what he would do the next time they stood in front of each other. Now here he was.

"What do you want?" he said, his voice sounding as alien to his own ears as it had done in the café.

"I wanted to see you," Jack Poole said, spreading his arms wide. He began to move towards Poole, his smile wide.

Brock moved between them. "Mr Poole, I think you

should leave."

"Oh, do you? So you're the new surrogate dad, are you?"

"No, I'm his new bloody boss, and I'll have half of the police in Addervale down on your back if I catch you within one hundred yards of this man," Brock snarled.

Jack Poole's eyes narrowed, though the smile stayed fixed on his face. Movement from behind the group made them turn to see two men who had positioned themselves on the pavement in front of them. Brock stared at them for a moment before turning back to Jack Poole.

"Well," Jack said, his eyes fixed on Poole, who was still staring at him, his mouth hanging slightly open. "If you're my son's boss then I best not get on the wrong side of you, eh?"

He stepped towards Brock, who stiffened and extended his hand. Brock glanced at Poole before exhaling through his nose and shaking Jack's hand firmly.

"Very nice to meet you, Inspector Brock," Jack said. "I plan to settle down around here, so I'm sure we'll be seeing more of each other." He turned to Guy. "We've got a lot of catching up to do, Guy." His face softened. "But I know it's going to take time. I just wanted you to know that I'm back. The ball's in your court now." He gave him a small, pained smile and then walked past them and carried on down the street, the men who had been standing there falling into step behind him.

Guy pulled his phone from his pocket, his hands shaking.

"Mum?" he said as his call was answered, his voice desperate.

"Guy? What's wrong?"

"Are you OK?"

"Of course I am. What's happened?" She sounded panicked now.

"I saw him, Mum. I saw Dad."

BROCK HAD INSISTED that they still go to the pub, and so they had swung by Poole's flat and picked his mother up along the way.

"I'm telling you, alcohol is the best thing for a shock," the inspector was saying as he leaned on the bar of The Mop & Bucket, waiting for their drinks.

"You think alcohol is the best thing for everything," Laura said, her eyes rolling.

"Well I for one appreciate it," Jenny Poole said, her eyes glassy from the tears she had shed while waiting, alone, for Guy to reach her. She had recovered now and had a light smile on her lips. "I have to say that I feel like I need a bloody good drink."

"Well, I'll drink to that," Laura said. "And don't worry, these are on Sam, and ..." she said, her voice rising to cover his protests, "we'll pay for a taxi home for everyone."

Brock huffed but said nothing.

They settled around the table that Poole had sat on with Sanita and the others from the station previously. An awkward silence spread about them as though no one knew whether to talk about what had happened or not.

"So," Laura said, breaking the ice. "What do you do, Jenny?"

"I run an eBay shop selling crystals, good luck charms, essential oils, things like that."

"Oh, you'd love this new exhibit we've got at the museum. It's full of African folk art and loads of it is about spiritual healing."

Poole watched his mother's eyes light up as she enthusiastically got stuck into the subject. He caught Brock smiling at him.

"Not the traditional celebratory case-closed pint," he said, leaning across the table to him. "But do you know, I've found that even when you win it often doesn't feel like it."

Poole nodded. "I know what you mean, sir."

"The good thing is," Brock continued, smiling, "there's always the mystery of what's coming next, isn't there?" He nodded over Poole's shoulder. He turned to see Constable Sanita Sanders enter the pub with the others from the station. She saw them and waved before moving to the bar.

Poole turned back, grinning, and tried to bury his blush in his pint glass.

CHAPTER 19

It was three whole days before they could properly question Sandra Hooke. She had been treated for jimsonweed poisoning which had apparently been administered in the vicar's herbal tea, probably for years.

The psychiatric evaluations had indicated that there would be a long road to recovery.

She sat now in the small interview room with a lawyer on one side and a psychiatrist on the other and fiddled nervously with the tissue in her hand.

"Sandra, we need to know what happened the night Charlie Lake died. The truth," Brock said softly.

She bit her bottom lip hard. Poole could see that this was a habit these days; it was red raw.

"Charlie didn't really fit in with the rest of us," she said in a small voice. "We were all young, experimenting, but he didn't want any part of that. Charlotte would take anything under the sun to get high. It was like, the tamer her parents were, the wilder she was. Henry was obsessed with her." She swallowed and tore the tissue into small strips. "And I liked Henry." She shook her head violently. "It was all just such a mess. That night we fell out in The Bell, Charlie was giving us his usual speech about how we shouldn't be so reckless. We all told him to sod off and went out."

She raised her head, her eyes closed, and took a deep breath.

"We were out in Bexford until late, drinking and egging each other on until we were smashed. Charlotte was completely out of it. She started saying we should teach Charlie a lesson, scare him. We called him and told him he should sneak out and meet us on the green. We all thought it was hilarious." Her voice caught in the back of her throat and she took the small cup of water in front of her and sipped at it.

"I was driving. Henry and Charlotte said I was the most sober so I had to. We were going to scare Charlie —just scare him," she said. Her voice was flat now, as though her mind had switched off and her voice was working automatically.

"He was there on the green and I headed for him. I can remember his face. He wasn't scared, he just looked annoyed. He knew it was all just a joke. I think that's what annoyed Charlotte, that he wasn't scared. She leaned over and grabbed the wheel and I couldn't turn away, and then—" She broke off and looked down at the tissue which had now been shredded.

"Charlotte ran off home. Henry and I didn't know

what to do. So we went to Dad. He convinced Henry to say he'd been driving." She looked up at Brock sharply. "Do you know who David Lake is?"

Brock nodded. "We do."

"Well, then you'll know why Dad was trying to protect me. He knew what David would do to whoever killed his son. Henry knew his gran would be screwed if she lost her cottage and Dad could kick her out if he wanted. Dad said he'd look after her, make sure she had the best care. Henry gave in." She paused and stirred the scraps of tissue with her finger. "I think he did it for me as much as anything," she said quietly.

"Wasn't your dad worried that Henry would say something?"

"He visited Henry all the time, told him how his mum was. I think he thought David Lake would have him killed somehow, but he never did."

"Did David Lake ever threaten you?" Brock said.

She shook her head. "He came to see me not long afterwards, but he saw I was unwell..." She paused again and frowned. "I think he preferred to see me suffer like that."

"And can you remember what happened when Henry was released?"

She shook her head. "He was angry. He came to the house, ranting. Said Dad had killed Edie. I went back out later to find him and I saw him on the green, but he sent me away. I—I don't know," she said, shaking her head again.

"I think we might have had enough for now," the psychiatrist said, giving a stern look to the inspector.

"One more question," Brock said. "Malcolm Paget."

"He was shouting about the crowbar Dad had. He —he hit him with it and we had to move him. I..."

"I really think this is enough," the psychiatrist said, standing up. Brock nodded as Sandra Hooke shook in front of them, her eyes staring at the wall.

A few minutes later, Brock and Poole were back in their office.

"If Edie Gaven hadn't died when she did, then maybe all of this wouldn't have happened," Poole said, leaning back in his chair.

"I've been thinking about that," Brock said, placing his hands behind his head. "Did you know that the germs that cause pneumonia are contagious, Poole?"

"Contagious? No, I didn't, sir."

"The vicar was volunteering at the hospital and apparently in the week before Edie was admitted, had been attending an elderly gentleman who had pneumonia."

"Are you suggesting he might have deliberately infected Edie?!" Poole said, sitting up straight.

"Who knows?" Brock answered. "But maybe he thought Henry would tell his gran the truth once he got out of prison?"

Poole sighed, trying to take this in.

"Have you heard anything else from your dad?" Brock asked, catching Poole by surprise. He felt the familiar iron ball in his stomach that appeared every time he thought of his father.

"No," he answered.

"Good," Brock said, standing up and clapping his hands together. "How about we go and get a sandwich at Sal's?"

Poole grinned. "Sounds good."

Brock passed him his coat from the stand and put his own before pointing one large finger at Poole. "Just don't tell Laura."

I hope you enjoyed this book, if you did, please consider leaving a review!

For news on upcoming books visit agbarnett.com and join A.G.Barnett's newsletter to get new release alerts.

Don't miss the next book in the series... *A Staged Death*... Turn the page for the first chapter!

A STAGED DEATH

Ronald Smith hopped from one foot to the other nervously, his small frame a bundle of excited energy. Today was the day he was going to hit the big time.

As he stood in the wings he could almost feel the excitement in the air, as though an electric current was zigzagging its way around the theatre and giving every person inside it a jolt of adrenaline.

He'd been working on the hit TV show *Foul Murder* for three years now, but his role as the pathologist consultant hadn't brought him the notoriety he craved. In fact, his colleagues openly mocked his involvement. This was what had spurred him on to request a walk-on part at least six times, all of which had been declined.

Then he had had his big idea.

There would be no more scoffing once they realised

he was behind the greatest publicity the show had ever had.

His beady eyes scoured the audience that filled the small theatre. Various representatives from the national press's entertainment sections filled the first row. They quaffed their free champagne and laughed loudly as they swapped stories about whoever the latest celebrity to have an affair was. Part of the deal for tonight was that it was strictly a no-camera, no-recording deal. This was a live spectacle and wasn't going to turn into some YouTube video. The entire audience had been searched and their devices removed upon entry. If anything, it had added to the buzz and excitement in the place.

The crowd hushed as a low bass tone rose from the huge speakers that hung discreetly from the walls. Ronald Smith basked in the glow of it all. This was it. This was his moment.

* * *

Poole walked behind Brock in a state of confusion. He knew that the inspector despised Ronald Smith. Though, to be fair to the big man, he hadn't yet met anyone who didn't despise Ronald Smith. The pathologist was a weasel, and that was giving a bad name to weasels. So why, then, had the inspector accepted this invitation to come to a launch event for the new series of *Foul Murder*? Whatever the reason, Poole was glad. He secretly enjoyed *Foul Murder* but would never pass this fact on to Brock, who would no doubt see it as a betrayal, and especially not to Ronald Smith, who would gloat like the toad he was.

He had been surprised when he had heard that the series six opener was being filmed in his new home county of Addervale, and even more surprised when he had heard that they were going to stage a press event announcing the return of the show in his new home town of Bexford.

Ronald Smith, of course, had been bragging relentlessly ever since the announcement had been made, casually mentioning where he planned to take the stars to dinner when they arrived, saying it had been his influence that had persuaded the producer to film the opening of the new series in Addervale.

Of everyone in the station, it had been Inspector Brock that Ronald had decided to invite. Poole could only guess that the intention was to rub his nose in Ronald's proximity to fame. Brock had insisted on his wife Laura having a ticket as well, but when Ronald had obliged, Laura had been caught up with work and so Poole had been invited in her place.

The truth was, Poole was in a bad mood. He had had a run in with Detective Sergeant Anderson earlier that day, and as always, he had gotten under his skin.

Anderson had been boasting about being assigned to a murder case, apparently over Brock and Poole. He had also bragged about how close the relationship between his superior, Inspector Sharp, and Chief Inspector Tannock was.

"Sir?" Poole asked as they passed through Bedford's

main town square, the lights shining off the cobbles that covered its centre. "What's the deal with Chief Inspector Tannock?"

Brock looked curiously sideways at him. "What do you mean?"

"I mean, I've barely ever even seen the man. He doesn't ever seem to be in the office."

Brock sighed and pulled a battered bag of boiled sweets from his jacket pocket and offered the bag to Poole, who shook his head.

"Have you ever seen those old war films where the generals sit on top of the hill drinking tea while the men are down at the bottom, running into the gunfire and generally having a terrible time of it?" Brock said, popping a sweet into his mouth before returning the packet.

"Yes?" Poole answered, confused.

"Chief Inspector Tannock is one of those generals on the hill, and we're all down at the bottom getting shot at."

"Oh, right, sir."

"But not for long," Brock added. "He's retiring soon. It's going to be a shock to old Sharp, I can tell you."

"Why's that, sir?"

"Well, him and Tannock go way back—old army buddies. I think they're what people refer to as 'part of the old boys' club', and when someone new comes in I think Sharp is in for a rude awakening."

"Right. Thanks, sir," Poole said, smiling. He was suddenly feeling much better about things.

They entered a side street, and after a few hundred metres, the New Theatre loomed. Its golden-coloured stone shone in the spotlights that surrounded it.

"Here we are then, Poole," Brock said, pushing at the large door and stepping inside.

The foyer was empty. They quickly crossed it, heading towards a bored-looking teenage girl who stood behind a podium.

"You're late," she said, sighing as Brock handed her the tickets. "But they haven't started yet."

The inspector grunted and marched on through the double doors, which opened with a soft, swoosh.

The lights were darkening as they stepped through into the theatre and music was beginning to pulse around the now hushed space. They took two seats in the last row, the only area where seats were still available, and settled down to watch the show.

The screen at the back of the stage lit up with the intro sequence to the show. The theme music kicked in, causing the crowd to whoop and cheer.

"Bloody hell," Brock muttered.

Poole turned to him, expecting to see the usual gruff expression, but instead, something else played across his expressive face. Poole was sure he was mistaken, but it looked as though there was a flicker of enjoyment there.

A man bounced onto the stage followed by a group of

four people who all waved as the crowd applauded and whooped at an even greater volume. The man leading the group wore a bright blue suit with a crisp white shirt, its oversized collar jutting up, framing his stubble jaw.

Poole recognised him instantly as Jarvis Alvarado, star of the show and heartthrob of the nation. The rest of the number he recognised as fellow cast members. They took up positions on metal stools that had been whisked onto the stage by scurrying black-clothed figures.

Alvarado stood in front of them, a microphone in his hand.

"Ladies and gentlemen!" he said, arms wide, his voice reverberating through the large speakers that hung from the walls.

"It is so good to see you all here tonight," he continued, "for what I'm sure is going to be the beginning of something very special!"

The crowd applauded as he flashed a set of bright white and perfect teeth that seemed to glow against his olive skin. The theme tune was still blaring from the speakers, its deep bass and heavy guitars sounding more appropriate for Wembley Stadium than the New Theatre at Bexford.

"And for you lovely people here tonight," he continued, "we have something very special indeed!"

He moved to the side of the stage and gestured to the heavens, both arms stretched out before him. There was a movement from above the stage and the crowd gasped as an exact replica of the office the *Foul Murder* team used on the show was lowered towards the stage floor behind the arranged cast.

Jarvis waved his arms to indicate he wanted more cheers from the crowd, and they responded with enthusiasm.

"Tonight, we will perform the opening scene from the first episode live just for you!"

The crowd cheered again, but the sound changed to a shocked intake of breath as the lights blinked out across the entire theatre.

"Sir?" Poole said, turning to his left and not seeing Brock, though he knew he must only be inches from him.

Brock's familiar gruff voice came back from the black. "Don't worry, Poole, I've got a feeling this is all part of the act."

Poole listened to the excited chatter of the crowd and tried to get his eyes to adjust, but it was no use. The place was built to not let natural light in.

"It could just be a power cut, sir," Poole continued. "Maybe an electrical problem?"

"Just wait, Poole," Brock's voice came back. "Never believe anything with these showbiz types."

Poole smiled in the dark. There didn't seem to be many people that Brock trusted. He had an in-built instinct that everyone was trying to pull the wool over his eyes.

The lights burst on with a brightness that made everyone in the audience blink furiously.

A piercing scream cut through the murmuring from

the stage. A woman from the cast had risen from her stool and was pointing at the prone figure of Jarvis Alvarado, who lay sprawled at the front of the stage with a pool of blood spreading in a halo around his head.

Poole jumped to his feet. There were more screams now, they broke out all around as people pointed as people rushed onto the stage.

"Sit down, Poole," Brock said, folding his arms. "This is all part of it."

"Are you sure, sir?" Poole said, his eyes locked on the pool of blood.

"Of course it is! I mean, come on. The lights go out and then a murder occurs in those few minutes? It's like something for some terrible murder mystery rubbish on TV, which is exactly what this is!"

Poole sat down again uncertainly as panicked figures shouted for help on stage.

"And here he comes," Brock said. Poole followed his finger to the right of the stage, where the small ferrety figure of Ronald Smith was scurrying towards the small gathering of people. "No wonder he invited us here," Brock said with a derisive snort. "The little git's got his own walk-on part."

They watched as Ronald Smith bent over Jarvis Alvarado. Poole noticed for the first time that the crowd that had gathered on stage were stood in a perfect semicircle, allowing the audience to see exactly what was going on. He smiled to himself again. The inspector was right: this was all part of the show. They hadn't even dropped the curtain to hide the scene for the audience or made an announcement. This was all part of the drama. He leaned back, deciding to enjoy it all.

They watched as Ronald Smith fussed over the prone figure, theatrically taking his pulse and then looking into his eyes with a small torch. Then he paused and stood up, staggering slightly. He turned wildly around at the people on stage, who were now all staring at him. He looked out into the audience and shielded his eyes from the lights and he shouted in his squeak of a voice.

"Brock!"

The inspector jumped up next to Poole and began pulling him up and pushing him into the aisle.

"You're not going down there, are you?!" Poole said, surprised at the sudden change of heart.

"Yes, I bloody am," Brock answered, bustling them both down the aisle. "Because I know Ronald Smith, and I know there's no way on earth he's that good an actor."

BOOKS BY A.G. BARNETT

BROCK & POOLE MYSTERIES

An Occupied Grave

A Staged Death

When the Party Died